Tied to Him

Tied to Him

DELILAH FAWKES

DEDICATION

Dedicated to my wonderful fans, who make these stories possible, and to people fighting to give everyone a chance at a happy ending. Your love for others is truly inspirational.

Tied to Him

CHAPTER 1

"How bad is it, really? And don't sugar coat it. Give it to me straight."

My campaign advisor brushed non-existent lint off her blazer before answering. Not a good sign. She only did that when she was stalling for time.

"Well, Jackson, honestly… It's not great. TMZ says they have a woman who's confessing you tied her up and spanked her at some club five years ago. It's pretty juicy stuff, although there's obviously no proof other than her word. Regardless, they're running with it, the rat bastards."

I sighed, rubbing the bridge of my nose. A headache throbbed behind my eyes.

So this is it. My past finally caught up with me.

"There couldn't be a worse time for this, Lisa. I just announced my candidacy for Governor, for God's sake!"

"Tell me about it," she said. "Just square with me on this one, Jacks. Do we have anything to worry about here? Is what she saying true?"

My thoughts wandered back to the club I frequented with my brother, Max. We were both young and reckless and hungry to scratch the itch that afflicted the both of us the same way and had our whole lives. Going to The Knot was a weekly event in those days… But that was all behind me.

Sure, I had my affairs, but now that I was older and wiser I'd learned a thing or two about discretion. Especially now that I was running for office. The last thing this campaign needed was some trumped-up scandal sinking us before we even got started.

I decided to be honest. If anyone could help me out of this, it was Lisa. She was the best, the cornerstone of any campaign she was hired for, which is why I hired her. If you wanted to get elected, you needed Lisa Stoneworth on your side.

"Years ago, I was into that scene, yes. I very well could have played with that woman. But I've been out since before I took the job as D.A."

Lisa sat back, her lips pursed as she gave me her trademark cool, assessing look.

"Well, shit."

I let her digest this new information, watching as the gears turned, her eyes far away behind her heavy-framed glasses.

"Tell me what to do to fix this, and I'll do it. You know I'll do whatever you advise to make this right."

She rubbed her chin and sat forward again, looking me over again. A hint of amusement showed in the twist of her lips, and suddenly, I didn't know if I wanted to hear whatever she was about to suggest. From the look on her face, I suspected I wouldn't like it.

"You'll do anything, Jacks? Because I think I know how we can fix this if you're willing to play ball. Do you trust me?"

My muscles tensed as I waited for the hammer to fall.

"You know I do."

"Then comb your hair and come with me." She rose to her feet. "We're going to find you a respectable woman. Fast."

I pinched the bridge of my nose and followed her to the door. What had I just agreed to do?

CHAPTER 2

"Chili again?"

I rolled my eyes, then grinned at Jordan. The kid looked like he'd grown two inches this week. Hell, maybe had. Since I started cooking one meal per week at the youth shelter, I'd seen him sprout like a weed.

"I thought you loved my chili."

I crossed my arms across my apron and pouted. Jordan laughed. He wasn't buying it.

"You know it's supposed to have beans, right? That's how grandma always made it."

"Well, I can't help it if your grandma doesn't know how to make chili."

I ladled a steaming portion into his bowl with a flourish. He snorted in disbelief, his basketball in its usual place, tucked under his skinny arm.

"Listen, there is a major chili feud happening across America that you just don't know about, kiddo. Some say beans, some say serve it over spaghetti, but you don't listen to those people because they're wrong. There's only one way to make chili, and that's with meat, baby. I don't have time to be messing around with inferior chili."

"How do you know you're not the one with the dumb chili?"

I shook my head, sighing in mock exasperation.

"Simple, Jordan. This is straight up Texas-style, chili reserved for stone cold badasses. Outlaws. Sheriffs. Wyatt Earp. Peppers, tomatoes, dead cows and that's it. Question is, can you handle it?"

He laughed and grabbed his bowl away from me.

"Don't forget your cornbread."

I tucked a big square of it into his hand in the nick of time. He ran back to the table where his friends sat, laughing and talking, leaning over their steaming bowls for warmth.

I grinned, a pang of bitter sweetness growing inside of me as I watched them. This was probably the only meal these kids would have all day, which is why I tried to stuff them full of hearty food whenever I could. They were still growing, and the streets were cold this time of year for those not lucky enough to be in the system.

We had a mixture of homeless and foster that showed up at this youth center, seeking shelter, basic nutrition and hygiene supplies, and more often than not, just one moment with people they felt safe around. All of those things were rare for these kids. Something I understood all too well.

A small, thin girl approached the food line, her eyes downcast.

"Are you new here, honey?"

I ladled and she nodded, still not making eye contact. Her blonde hair was dirty, her pink sweatshirt hanging off her like she was no more substantial than a clothes hanger.

"I'm Rose," I said.

I handed her the bowl with a big block of my famous cornbread. She looked up briefly, her lips a thin line.

"It gets better," I said gently. "I promise. Stick around, okay?"

She looked away, but I saw the tension in her little shoulders slacken. She snuck a glance over her shoulder at me as she walked away, and I smiled.

All I could do was try to make the new kids feel warm and welcome. The rest was up to them to trust we'd be there for them. That is, if we could get the funding. The center was in the red again, despite our best efforts to fundraise. If something didn't change soon, they'd be in serious danger of closing the doors.

And that was the scariest part. Because as much as I wanted to help each and every kid who needed me, it came down to whether the resources to keep this place running existed. If the programs got shut down, the center would have to turn kids away, and then the thin trust we'd built, the hope we'd given them, would be destroyed.

I knew first hand how important it was to be able to trust. Once that was lost, you never forgot, and you never forgave.

I sighed and stirred the kettle of chili, watching the kids eat and laugh, the sound of their voices soothing my fears about this place, at least for the moment. I shook my head, and went back to cutting squares of cornbread.

There were more kids to feed, and I had to be ready.

CHAPTER 3

"What's wrong with that one?"

I glared at Lisa as she and I spied on the women bustling about the campaign headquarters, both of us staring through the blinds of the break room window.

"Is she too young for you, like the others? Or are you just getting cold feet about this little plan of mine?"

She frowned over her glasses at me like a disapproving mother.

"First off, I don't think it would be very wise of us to choose someone in college, no matter how great their scholarships are. We're trying to make me look respectable—your words—so looking like I'm robbing the cradle is probably not the way to go. And secondly, have you talked to Nancy over there? Ever?"

Lisa took another look at the thirty-something blonde bending over the filing cabinets.

"Well, okay, not really. But her file says she's a Rhodes Scholar and her family owns the local hospital…"

"Let's just say that the other day I asked how the organization for the fundraiser was going, and she hit me with a stack of spreadsheets."

"She…?"

"Smacked me in the chest with the spreadsheets. Then, she said, and I quote, 'It would go a lot better if you didn't keep nagging me.' It was the first time I'd ever spoken to her."

Lisa mulled this over.

"Okay, so she's a little nuts. Understood. Good catch, Jacks."

I sighed, and ran my hands through my short, dark hair. It was late, and we were still stuck in the office, trying to figure out how to enact Lisa's harebrained plan. She refused to let me leave until we had some idea of where to start, and I could understand why. Not only my reputation was on the line. If this scandal ruined me, her record for getting people elected would be collateral damage.

"Everyone else here is married or one of those lesbians," she said.

The door to the break room opened, and a slender woman with a ponytail came in, holding a salad.

"Evening, Lisa. Mr. Pierce," she said.

"Hey, Sara," Lisa said. She raised her eyebrows at me. "How's the wife? Still in the honeymoon phase?"

Sara giggled and blushed.

"We're just fine, thank you. And thanks for the time off. I'm ready to get back to helping you get elected, Sir."

"Thank you, Sara," I said, smiling back. "I appreciate what you do here."

She put her salad in the fridge and left. Lisa turned to me and frowned.

"We've got to get some fresh meat up in here."

I ran a hand over my face. I needed coffee. Coffee and a miracle if we were going to pull this off.

"Why don't we drop by some places where a likely candidate might go? Try to find someone in their natural habitat?"

"Like where? A kid's cancer ward?"

Lisa pursed her lips, and I could tell she was mulling it over.

"That's messed up, Lisa. I don't even have a kid. What am I going to do in a kid's cancer…?" I sighed. "God. No, let's check out local charities and youth organizations. I've been meaning to get some volunteering in anyway, but we've been so slammed, I haven't been able to get out. It would be a perfect opportunity."

She tapped her bottom lip, then grinned at me in a way that reminded me of an eagle swooping down on a field mouse.

"Brilliant. We can get some media coverage while you're at it. Make sure you roll up your shirtsleeves when you-"

"No media," I said.

My head was really pounding now. I needed to get out of here.

"I want to make the rounds myself. Alone. I'll call you if I come up with anything."

"Alright, but it's the perfect opportunity…"

"Lisa, enough. I just want to do some good before I sign all my free time over to you. Is that all right? Am I allowed to do volunteer work any more, or just the crazy shit you want me to do?"

She shook her head, tsking at me.

"Is that any way to talk? Especially to the woman who will plan your perfect wedding? I'm practically mother of the groom here, and this is the thanks I get."

I bit my tongue before I could say something I'd really regret.

Just get elected, Jackson, and you can get back to your roots. You can focus on education reform, just like you wanted. Get things done. Change lives for the better…

But, to do that, I knew I'd have to play ball. That's just the way it is in politics. The people who can endure the bullshit rise to the top, and that's where you did the real good; made the changes that mattered. But until then, you had to put up with a whole lot of… well… shit.

"Go get 'em, Romeo," Lisa said, clapping me on the back. "With your money and your looks, you should be able to bag a good one, no problem."

I clenched my fists and left the break room, slamming the door closed behind me.

CHAPTER 4

The next week, I decided to go all out and make Cajon mac and cheese with Andouille sausage. I had the day off from my data entry job and spent a tiring but soothing afternoon doing my favorite thing—cooking enough food for an army.

When the kids arrived at the center that night, Jordan gave it a suspicious sniff, then ate with gusto, grinning around a mouthful of noodles. I took that as a sign of approval, putting the recipe on my mental list of hits with the regulars.

As I was serving the last of the teens, a strange man walked in, chatting with Kathy, the volunteer coordinator. I frowned, taking in his expensive shoes and designer jeans, even though he was obviously trying for a casual look, but when I took in his handsome face, I paused mid-scoop, sucking in a breath.

It was Jackson Pierce, the former D.A. now running for Governor. The billionaire who actually seemed to give a damn about education for the underprivileged. Or so he claimed in his television spots. I'd been burned too many times by political wannabes to be anything but skeptical. But here he was, despite my wariness, and not a single member of the press anywhere to be seen.

If this isn't a photo op, why is he here?

"You okay, Rose?"

Joaquin stared at me, his plate held out in front of him. I shook my head and scooped him a heaping helping.

"Just fine, hon. Keep it moving, guys."

I looked up again as I worked, and saw him moving toward us, his dark eyes locked on mine. Kathy grinned from ear to ear, telling him about the facilities here as well as the food programs.

"And this is one of our super stars, Rose Turner," she said, gesturing at me like Vanna White showing off a vowel.

"Pleasure to meet you, Rose," he said, extending his hand. "Jackson Pierce."

"I, uh…"

I hadn't expected him to be this handsome up close in real life. In person, he was like a magnetic force, his face chiseled and fiercely handsome, his gaze powerful and hypnotic. His hair was short, but carefully tousled, like he'd just rolled out of bed after a bout of lovemaking. I felt the heat creeping up into my cheeks, and realized I must be staring like an idiot.

"I, um, don't know about super star, but, yeah… Nice to meet you, too, Mr. Pierce."

Get it together, Rose. You sound like a star-struck little girl.

"Call me Jackson," he said.

He smiled, one dimple showing, and I almost dropped the spoon.

"Jackson here volunteered to help us out tonight, and I'm afraid I've been gabbing his ear off. We've almost missed dinner completely!"

She tittered, staring up at Jackson Pierce like a puppy dog in a lavender sweater set.

"Oh, but you can still serve these last few kids, and I'm sure Rose would love it if you'd help her with the clean up."

Him? Washing dishes and hauling garbage?

"Sure thing," he said. "Happy to help wherever you want me."

With another smile, Kathy squeezed his arm and left us alone. Feeling like I was in some kind of stress dream, I handed him a plastic apron and a serving spoon. He grinned, flashing straight, white teeth, and I swallowed hard. I suddenly wished I'd taken more time with my appearance today, but that was silly. My jeans, faded t-shirt, and bandana-covered hair made sense for the job at hand.

That's what was important. Not impressing some strange man. No matter how good-looking he was.

I cleared my throat.

"I give the kids a big scoop, like this," I said, holding up a heaping spoonful. "This could be the only time they eat today, and I always make more than enough, so don't worry about running out."

"You made this?"

He smiled at me, tying his apron on. I couldn't help but notice how firm his butt looked in those jeans.

He must work out...

"I cook once a week for this group. More if I'm able to get time off from work. But it's no big deal. I love to cook, but I don't have anyone at home to try new recipes on."

He nodded, a half smile on his face as he looked me over, approval flashing in his eyes.

I looked away, cursing inwardly at the way I felt beneath that scrutinizing gaze, but snapped back to attention as a group of gangly girls came through the line. The small girl from last week was back, hanging back from the others. Jackson and I scooped noodles and sausage up for the crowd, but when the last girl approached, she passed by Jackson, stopping in front of me. She held her plate up, her eyes darting upward to meet mine, before lowering again.

I smiled down at her and served her up a steaming portion.

"I'm glad to see you back," I said. "You know my name, but now that we're practically old friends, maybe you can tell me yours?"

"Lana," she said. Her voice was barely more than a whisper.

"Pleasure to meet you, Lana. Hope to see you back here soon."

I winked at her, and she gave me a shy smile before scurrying off to eat. Jackson was watching me when I looked back up.

"You've got a way with the shy ones."

I shrugged.

"I was shy myself. It helps if you know someone notices you, but for the right reasons. Not just to put you down."

He glanced back at Lana, sitting at the edge of the table, away from the others. She ate with vigor, her cheeks puffing out as she packed them full.

"I can't imagine what it's like for them," he said. "That's why I'm here. I want to be closer to the community's problems so I know what's needed to solve them."

I frowned a little at his words. Of course he didn't know what it was like. He was privileged from birth. He'd probably never been hungry a day in his life, unlike so many Americans, it hurt to think about it.

I wondered what he thought of this place. Was this just an attraction for him? A zoo where he could view the poor, then go home and fall asleep on a silk pillow, feeling good about himself?

"Have you volunteered before?" I said.

"I usually work at the men's shelter up on Weston Street, or sometimes the women's crisis center, but I wanted to branch out tonight. There's a lot I don't know about what the state does in terms of outreach for the youth."

I tried to hide my surprise by turning my attention to stirring the mac and cheese, mixing the sausage into the next spoonful. Maybe this guy wasn't a rich bitch after all, or maybe he was just leading me on.

"Not a lot of politicians do that," I said. "Not unless there's a picture being taken. They stay one minute, shake some hands, snap some pics, serve a couple of bowls of soup, and then they're gone, like a whirlwind blowing through. The kids don't know what to think."

His face hardened as he looked over the crowd of kids before us, some as young as eleven, many in their mid-to-late teens. Despite a mixture of homeless and kids in the system, they had one thing in common: they were all dirty, all unloved, all here for a hot meal they couldn't get anywhere else. Taking what they could get in this cold city. Doing the best with the hand they'd been dealt.

"Well," he said. "After the kids are served, just give me a job. I think you'll find I'm a hard worker, so don't be shy."

Shame colored my cheeks. I'd insulted him before he even had a chance to prove his character.

Who's the bitch now, Rose?

A powerful man like this might be a good friend for the youth center to have, and I could chase him away if I didn't adjust my attitude. I watched the crowd, trying to focus on just breathing, waiting for the next wave of kids to arrive.

I had to keep it together, at least for one night. How hard could it possibly be?

CHAPTER 5

I couldn't believe my luck.

She was almost too perfect—everything I needed for Lisa's plan to work.

Not only was Rose Turner extremely dedicated to her cause, she was well-liked by the kids, passionate, and beautiful. Her short dark hair escaped beneath the flap of her bandana, making her look like a modern day Rosie the Riveter, her athletic body distracting in faded jeans and a tight t-shirt. Her eyes lit up when she spoke, her words simple, but her tone betraying her excitement for what she did. I could tell how much she loved this place, and when she looked out over the youth she served, she was absolutely radiant.

The public would fall head-over-heels in love with her. Which was exactly what I needed.

After the last kids were served, I carried the chafing dishes into the kitchen and got to work spraying and scrubbing. Rose wrapped up leftovers beside me and stored them in the youth center's meager fridge.

She was right—there was no danger of running out of food tonight, although from what Kathy told me on the tour, they usually had to limit portions when she wasn't available. There just weren't enough volunteers, and definitely not enough funding. Where did a working class woman like her get the money to cook for so many? Even though money had never been a problem for me, I made sure I knew how much things cost for the average household, and a meal for so many would be hard to pull off for most people once a month, much less once a week. Rose must be sacrificing her own standard of living to make this work.

From time to time as we worked, I saw her sneaking glances at me. Sizing me up. She was sharp as a tack, I could tell, and she didn't know what to make of me yet. I couldn't blame her. Politicians weren't exactly known for being trustworthy and transparent.

"Tell me, Rose," I said, toweling off the last of the serving spoons. "Where'd you learn to cook like that? Do you have a big family?"

She was quiet for a long moment, so long that I wondered if she'd heard me, but then her bright eyes met mine. For a flash, they held such deep sadness, I almost had to look away. But as quickly as the emotion came, her eyes hardened, and it was gone again. She looked away.

"Not really. I was an only child until I went into the system."

"Oh," I said. "You mean the foster system?"

"Mm hmm." She turned her back to me, scrubbing the countertops. "In some of the houses I stayed there were other kids, but I didn't really start cooking until…" She paused for a moment, her back muscles tensing. "Until later."

"Well, from the kids' reactions, you've got a real talent for it. I can't imagine planning a meal like this, much less executing it all by myself. I'd probably burn the kitchen down."

She turned to me and raised an eyebrow, but I thought I saw the hint of a smile in her eyes.

There it is. Pride in what she does. She knows she's good.

"These kids will eat anything," she said. "They're teenagers."

"Yeah, but kids are picky. They might eat it because they have to, but from the looks on their faces tonight, your food is something special. You go all out."

She did smile, then, a softness coming over her making her look delicate and feminine, despite the firm muscles I could see on her arms and the tall, fit build of her body. She was used to working hard, and it showed.

Beautiful, I thought. She really is different than other women I've met. There's something about her I can't quite put my finger on...

"Like I said earlier, I get to experiment on them is all. I find a new recipe, or I throw some stuff together at home, and I want to share it. They get enough of the regular cafeteria stuff like sandwiches and chicken nuggets, so I figure why not, right? Like Paul Prudhomme said, 'You don't need a silver fork to eat good food.' Oh..."

She stopped short, looking at me with wide eyes.

"I didn't mean-"

"It's okay," I said. I laughed at the look on her face. "I don't think being a billionaire is a protected class. Besides, I'm not offended in the least."

She looked down at her sneakers and let out a nervous laugh, then yanked her bandana down around her neck and ran her fingers roughly through her hair.

"I'm always putting my foot in my mouth. Honestly... I've never been around... someone like you before."

She looked up at me, her short hair wild and rough, and chewed her lip in a way that made my cock stir in my pants.

Whoa, there... Where did that come from?

"You make me nervous," she said.

I cleared my throat and tugged my apron strings a little looser.

"Just because I'm running for office doesn't mean I'm not a regular guy."

She crossed her arms and smirked at me now, one hip thrust sideways in a way that displayed exactly what she thought of that statement.

"Mm hmm. You're just a regular ol' billionaire who just happened to have a star career as a D.A. and are now trying to run my state. No biggie, right? Just one of the guys."

"Exactly," I said.

I chuckled at the look on her face. She was something else, indeed.

"Seriously, though, Rose… I know you can cook, and I see how much you love helping here, but how do you afford it? Is that rude to ask?"

She straightened up and stared at me, her jaw clenching for the space of a heartbeat.

"I have a job. This place is important, so I make it happen, okay? I'm good… We're good."

I licked my bottom lip, and noticed her eyes flick down to my mouth, then back up again, meeting my gaze.

"I'm not saying you're not making it happen. I'm just wondering… Would you be interested in another job? A much, much, better paying one than your current employment?"

"How do you know it's better paying? You don't even know what I do."

She was getting angry, and I could tell she was starting to view me as an outsider again. An intruder in her world. I had to talk fast, or I wouldn't have a chance to convince her of what I needed.

"How does five million dollars for a year of work sound?"

She raised a finger, her mouth already forming an argument, when she froze, mid-motion. Her eyes widened until I thought they might fall out, and her mouth worked, as if trying to speak, but her brain wouldn't provide the words.

It would have been funny, if my political career didn't hinge on this one moment. This one woman.

"A problem just popped up for me," I said, "and I need your help to make it go away. I probably should have asked this first, but, are you currently seeing anyone?"

That seemed to snap her out of it.

She reeled back until her butt hit the counter behind her, her eyebrow raising incredulously.

"What?"

"Well, the job would be highly unusual, and I'd need you to keep things absolutely confidential during the year you work for me. I also can't have you seeing anyone, or you won't be right for this position."

"I... What?"

"Rose, I can't tell you more details until I know you're interested. I can't disclose my problem to just anyone. I need you to sign a confidentiality agreement before I can tell you about what you'd be doing if you accept my job offer."

"But... did you say million?"

"Five million dollars. For one year working for me. It can all be yours, Rose, along with an unrestricted spending allowance during that year, lodging, health care—the whole enchilada. I will take excellent care of you."

I moved closer, and she didn't flinch away. I put my hands on her shoulders. This close, I could smell the soft scent of her shampoo, something fruity and sensual.

"If you take this job, Rose," I said, "You can do anything you'd like for the rest of you life with the right financial planning. You can make feeding these kids a full time job and live off the interest."

She looked up into my eyes, her breathing shallow, and I could see her trying to take this all in. What must this be like for her? A stranger offering her more money than she could ever make in a hundred years at a high-paying management job.

Life-changing money.

It was funny to think that an amount like this could simultaneously be so huge and so small, depending on who you are. I spent five million on a vacation home in Bora Bora smaller than the east wing of my estate here. I realized now I've only been there once.

I'd almost forgotten I owned it.

"What do you say? Are you willing to hear more?"

She opened her mouth, then closed it again, squeezing her eyes shut like she was harnessing her chi. She finally opened them and nodded.

"Excellent! I can have the confidentiality agreement drawn up immediately. Are you available tomorrow evening to meet?"

She nodded again, and a small squeak left her lips. I smiled and ran my hands over her shoulders.

"Good. Let me have your address, and I'll send a car for you at 7:00 p.m. We can discuss business over dinner."

I handed her my cell phone and she plugged in her information with trembling hands.

"Thank you," I said. "I appreciate you hearing me out."

I walked toward the back door, when I heard her release the breath she'd been holding.

"Wait."

I turned back. She had her hand on her hip again, her chin held high.

"Why me?"

I grinned and put my hand on the door handle.

"Because you're perfect."

I didn't wait to see her reaction, but I smiled as I stepped out into the cool, night air.

This was going to work. I could feel it.

CHAPTER 6

I didn't sleep that night.

Five million dollars? Who the hell offered five million dollars for a year's work? What the hell kind of job in what reality earned that kind of money?

The worst-case scenarios flew through my mind.

Did he want me to be his prostitute? Some kind of concubine situation?

That seemed unlikely. I wasn't exactly a stunning beauty, and besides, he could probably get several dozen gorgeous escorts for the year at a price like that. He could buy a freaking harem and a mountain of condoms, for all I knew. So, that possibility was out.

Did he want me to run drugs or something?

That didn't make sense, either, when I thought about it. I saw in an airplane movie that a kilo of coke was worth something like twenty grand… I'd have to smuggle two hundred and fifty kilos of coke to even break even at five million. And, frankly, it seemed unlikely that any human could put that many baggies up their butt in 365 days without suffering some serious consequences.

What else could he possibly want me to do for five million dollars?

Whack somebody? Rob a bank? Give him both my kidneys?

The whole situation was just insane.

But the more I thought about the sheer amount of money, the more I imagined what I could do with it. About how much my life and the life of these teens could change with just one million, much less five. Not only could I put two or three million in the bank and live off the interest and investments, like Jackson said, but I could fund several years of the meal program myself. I could start a yearly scholarship award just out of my personal funds, and if I could tempt investors or create some sort of self-renewing fundraising event...

The sky was the limit, and the possibilities, the responsibilities, of it were positively blowing my mind.

Before I finally drifted off sometime after 5 a.m., I remember thinking I'd probably choke a spotted owl if it meant I could make a lasting difference for these kids.

Whatever a man like Jackson Pierce wanted with me, I was determined to give it to him. I couldn't do anything else. Not when there were so many people I could help.

Not when I could do something lasting. Something with purpose. Something to make a little dent in all the bad in the world, even if it meant compromising my values to do it.

Because it would make a difference, I had to try.

I nodded off, wondering if I could still stand to look at myself in the mirror when all was said and done, and wondering if that really mattered, if just one kid's life was changed for the better because of something I did.

I slept peacefully, and for a few brief hours, I didn't dream.

The day sprinted by in a whirlwind of activities. I lived in a grubby studio apartment made smaller by the piles of paper and clothing I left everywhere I went. I spent the day cleaning furiously, doing laundry, mopping, all of the things I usually left until the last minute. I could just barely stand the thought of a billionaire seeing my place in the best of circumstances. Seeing it dirty was out of the question.

After everything was put away, it was time to figure out what to wear. What vibe did I want to give off here? Confident? Demure? I pondered if I should try to look sexy in case I needed to drive a hard bargain, but doubted I could pull it off if it came right down to it. Eventually, I settled for a pair of slacks and a loose-fitting blouse. I wanted to look professional but keep it comfortable. I was already sweating when the car arrived.

Instead of Mr. Pierce coming up to meet me, his driver rapped on my door, then escorted me to down to the street. My eyebrows raised when I saw the Bentley parked across from my apartment building, sticking out like a sore thumb in front of the Chinese take-out place.

This was too weird.

The driver opened the door for me and ushered me into a luxurious leather-upholstered back seat. He drove and I sat, lost in thought, wondering what other weird shit I'd probably see before the night was over. And where was my mysterious host? I didn't know you send a driver to fetch people and deliver them to you. I imagined a human-sized take-out bag complete with fortune cookie, and repressed a nervous giggle.

We drove up into the hills at the edge of the city, to a private road I hadn't realized existed until now. I caught flashes of houses between the trees, bigger than any house had a right to be. Mansions, I suppose... the word felt strange even in my mind. Who lived like this? And what did they do with all the space?

I had trouble enough buying furniture to fill my one-bedroom. I couldn't imagine trying to furnish a veritable castle.

We pulled into a long driveway, and I peered through the window, watching with growing discomfort as we passed long lines of sculpted hedges and approached an enormous brick estate, crouching like a monster on the top of the hill. Lush lawns stretched off into the distance, a dark line of trees marking the edge of the property. I imagined statues and fountains lurking in the shadows, and a dungeon full of rubies and gold. Maybe even a medieval torture device or two.

This whole scene was ridiculous.

What could a guy like this want from a girl like me? I was dying to know exactly what kind of work he had in mind, and the sooner

I found out, the better, before my imagination really ran away with me. I chewed a nail as we pulled into a round driveway and stopped before a pillared entranceway.

The driver opened my door, and I thanked him, stepping out into the pool of golden light coming from sconces beside the huge, wooden doors. I raised my hand to knock, wondering how anyone could possibly hear me in a place this big, when one of doors swung inward on its own.

"Good evening, Ms. Turner. Please come in. We've been expecting you."

A small man with a silver mustache grinned up at me, gesturing for me to enter. I gave him a tense smile and hustled inside, suddenly wishing I'd chosen something fancier to wear. Maybe a dress, or at least some high-heels. I felt like a pauper in a fairytale castle, wearing my finest tattered rags for the occasion. I smoothed down my slacks and tried to stand up straight. Smile like I wasn't freaking out right now.

Never let 'em see you sweat.

"Mr. Pierce is waiting in the study," he said. "If you would please follow me?"

I just had time to panic over the size of the chandelier in the echoing foyer, before following the butler up the grand staircase, down a long hallway and around several turns to get to the back of the mansion. He finally stopped in front of a mahogany door and knocked with a white-gloved hand.

He pushed it open.

"Ms. Turner, Sir."

"Thank you, Geoffrey."

Jackson Pierce sat behind a carved desk, the wood glowing warmly in the low light of his desk lamp. He wore a dark suit jacket, but the shirt beneath was unbuttoned, making him look almost rakish despite his opulent surroundings.

I smiled as I noticed the tiny American flag pin on his lapel.

So much for that bad boy image.

Geoffrey closed the door behind us, leaving us alone.

"Please have a seat, Rose. Thank you for coming tonight."

He gestured to the chair across from him, and I sat down, marveling as I did at the gorgeous floor-to-ceiling bookshelves that surrounded us. There was a ladder leaning against one of them, attached to a railing.

I'd always wanted to climb on one of those, and I vowed that if he got up to use the bathroom or something, I'd take it for a spin.

I remember watching Beauty and the Beast as a kid and drooling over that amazing library. This was smaller, but no less impressive. I wished I could check out his collection. What books would a man like Jackson Pierce collect? Philosophy and history texts? Maybe political texts and biographies of his favorite historical figures? Or would it be full of novels, maybe even guilty pleasures like dime store mysteries and titillating thrillers?

But, I wasn't here to explore his reading tastes, as much as I wanted to snoop. I turned to my host, hoping he hadn't noticed me eye-groping his books.

"You look lovely tonight, Rose."

I raised an eyebrow, feeling out of place again, as quickly as that. I tucked a strand of hair behind my ear and forced a smile.

"Thanks. Uh… You, too."

He laughed and leaned back in his chair.

"I guess we'll get down to it, then. I had my lawyer draft up a non-disclosure agreement regarding the meeting we're about to have. I'll need you to sign it before I can move forward. The job I'm offering is… Well, it's of a sensitive nature. I'm sure you understand."

He pushed a piece of paper across the desk to me, along with a pen that looked like it cost more than my car.

I didn't understand, but I was willing to play by his rules in order to hear what exactly he had in mind. The fact was, I was so curious, I couldn't resist, even if I had to sign a whole sheaf of documents to get him to spill the beans. Besides, a girl like me was great at keeping secrets. One more was no skin off my nose.

I signed, dated, and passed the paper back to him.

"Very good," he said.

He tented his fingers beneath his chin and eyed me over, his dark eyes twinkling with something like approval. I wasn't used to men staring at me this way, like I was a pleasant surprise, and it took all my strength not to fidget beneath that scrutinizing gaze. What did he want from me?

He didn't seem in any hurry to speak. I cleared my throat.

"Well, now that you've got me here, what are you going to do with me?"

I tried what I hoped was a breezy laugh, but the sound fell flat. Jackson stood and moved to a wet bar in the corner.

"Something to drink?"

Oh, thank God.

"Whiskey, if you've got it."

He smiled to himself and poured two glasses, neat. When he handed me my tumbler, his fingers grazed mine. A spark passed between us, and I sucked in a deep breath. There was something powerful about this man that was impossible to ignore. From the brief pause before he pulled back, I wondered if he felt something from me as well.

He sat back and sipped his whiskey, waiting until I tried mine to speak. It was very good. The smoothest I'd ever had. Of course.

I didn't want to know how much it cost.

"Now that you've signed the confidentiality agreement, I hope I can be blunt."

"Absolutely."

Finally, he'd come out with it. He was killing me with all this secrecy.

"I need a bride."

I choked mid-sip and tried not to shoot whiskey out my nose. When I finally managed to swallow, I stared at him, wondering what the fuck I'd just gotten myself into.

"Now, I know what you're thinking, Rose, but it's not like that. You know I'm running for Governor, so you should know how important keeping up appearances is for me in the coming months, correct?"

"Sure…"

This was getting weird. I wondered if I could find my way back out of this house if I needed to get away from him. But even then, how would I get home? I should have driven myself. Why didn't I have a contingency in case Jackson was a nutcase?

Shit.

"Recently rumors have come out about certain… well, certain preferences of mine, and I need someone wholesome, for lack of a better word, to marry me and pretend that our relationship is legitimate. My image needs repairing, and a marriage to an upstanding woman would go a long way toward doing just that. That's where you come in."

"So…" I began. "You need a fake wife to hide the fact that you're gay?"

Please, God, just be gay. Don't be a psycho killer or a kiddie diddler or something even worse.

He laughed. "I'm not gay, Rose."

I swallowed hard, wondering how fast I could get to the doorknob if I needed to.

"Then what do you need a beard for?"

"I…"

He looked at me, and this time, I sensed he was truly uncomfortable. It was odd to watch. He was so self-assured, before. So in control. I relaxed in my seat, realizing he was just as embarrassed by this whole thing as I was weirded out.

"You said you'd be blunt."

"Yes, well. Yes," he said. "That's only fair. I… I'm not ashamed of my past, but sometimes people think the worst when they hear… I don't want you to think the worst of me, Rose…"

I leaned closer.

"If I'm going to agree to this, I need to know what you're covering up."

He frowned, then drank the rest of his liquor in one swallow.

"Do you know what a Dominant is, Rose?"

"Like in Fifty Shades of Grey?"

A small smile crept onto his face again.

"Sort of, but not exactly. It's not like it's made out to be in the media. I have certain urges, and I used to act on them. I frequented a BDSM club in another city, and one of the women I knew from those days just came forward to the press. The rumors will be everywhere soon, and I need to run interference before thing spin out of control."

"By looking like a good little Boy Scout instead of the Marquis de Sade?"

I smirked at him. I wasn't sure about this whole dominant business, but I'd been so tense for a moment, waiting to hear his deep, dark secret, that anything but the worst was a relief. This whole situation was so surreal, I didn't know how to react. I was just glad he didn't say 'I have several community service workers buried in my basement.'

"Exactly." He sat back and sighed. "I need someone like you, Rose. Someone the public will love. Who the local community already knows as a 'moral' person. I need the glamour and romance of a wedding and the normality of a marriage to draw attention away from my past."

"I get it," I said. "You need to get them off your nuts until they forget about the whole thing, and it's back to business as usual."

He chuckled.

"That's one way of putting it."

"However, I think you're barking up the wrong tree."

I did squirm now, shifting in my chair. I couldn't help it. I knew what I'd done in my life. Where I'd been. What I had to do to survive. I'd stolen when I was young and hungry. Hoarded. Gotten into fights on the street. Taken things and hurt people. It was a long time ago, but sometimes, when I slept, I dreamed about those days. They haunted me.

"I'm not good," I said. "I've had my problems, too, you know... You need someone like Miss America... I'm... I don't know. I'm not what you're looking for."

"You're perfect," he said.

I looked up into his eyes. His gaze held me, the power of those two words growing as I saw the sincerity behind them.

"You don't even know me."

"I know enough. You volunteer every week, spending more money than you can afford to feed those kids, and you do it out of love. You don't just give the minimum to keep them full—you take care to make each meal special. They know you care, and everyone loves you because of it. Because of who you are and what you give."

I looked down at my hands, tracing my fingernails.

"It's not that big of a deal. I have the time…"

"I researched you today, Rose. You've won awards from the mayor for community service. Your co-workers in your office had nothing but glowing things to say, and the other volunteers at the center say you're the main reason some of the more at risk kids keep showing up, instead of turning to selling drugs to survive. Although speaking to all these people, there was one theme hit on again and again. You don't realize your own worth. You make an impact on people, Rose, but you're humble."

"You talked to all those people? People at my work…?"

"I was discreet, of course. I have a contact at the local newspaper. You were chosen as their Spotlight on Community subject this week. Congratulations."

He winked at me, and I stared back blankly. All of this information made me feel like a deer in the headlights.

"The point is, you are very good, Rose. No matter what you think of yourself, others are inspired by what they see in you. You are capable, passionate, and, if I may say, absolutely beautiful. You're perfect for the job."

He leaned across the table and covered my hand with his. His eyes burned into mine.

"I need you."

I took a deep breath, trying not to let my mind lock on to how good his hand felt on mine, how warm and strong and sensual it felt to be touched by him.

He thinks I'm good. That I'm beautiful.

"If I agree," I said. "How would this even work?"

He gave my hand a squeeze, and a little thrill shooting up my arm. He sat back and grinned.

"Yes, the details. If you agree to the position, we'll say we started dating the night we met at the youth center. I fell for you instantly and asked if you'd do me the honor of having dinner with me."

"You better not have said it like that, or I would have laughed in your face."

"Yes, well. I'm sure I was very charming," he said. "We'll make public appearances at regular intervals, wherever you'd like, make appearances at a few events of mine, and then I'll propose somewhere public so news of our engagement spreads quickly. We'll have a wedding soon after, and then, you'll move into my home."

"I'll... move in?"

"Of course," he said. He raised an eyebrow at me. "In the public eye, we'll be husband and wife. How would it look if you were always coming and going, but never staying over?"

I chewed the inside of my lip. What would it be like living with this man? In a place like this? Despite my apartment's shabbiness, and the terrible neighborhood, okay, and the constantly leaking radiator, I liked where I lived. It would be hard to leave, especially since I'd be leaving it behind for good if I bailed for an entire year. There's no way it would still be waiting for me when all this was over.

But after that, I'd have five million dollars.

"Okay, so if I agree, I'll be living here. Where will I be staying? A guest room?"

He looked at me again in that way of his, that way that made me think he was looking right through me, a little smile playing over his lips.

"The servants may talk. I'll need you to keep up the act even in my home. You'll stay in the master suite with me."

"Hey, listen," I said. "You may not know me, but I'm not the kind of girl who sleeps around, okay? If this is some kind of weird sex game to you-"

"Rose," he said. "Relax. Despite the oddness of the situation, I intend to keep it strictly professional. But we need to get the details right, or there won't be any point. If I'm paying five million dollars for your help, this needs to be flawless. The public has to believe. Everyone must believe."

I frowned at him. Could I trust him? Could I put myself in his hands for an entire year, even with the outlandish reward at the end of it all?

"I don't need your answer tonight. Think about it. I hoped we might have dinner together now that you're here, though. Get to know one another," he said. "I want you to ask me anything you'd like, and in turn I'd like to know more about you. We have to trust one another if we're going to do this. And if you decide to walk away, at least you'll have a free meal for your trouble. What do you say?"

Dinner? I'd completely forgotten about food, but at the mention, my stomach rumbled. How strange that even after this bizarre conversation, I could still think about eating.

"That would be nice," I said. "Thank you, Mr. Pierce."

"I believe I told you to call me Jackson."

He smiled at me over tented fingers.

"Thank you, Jackson."

I let him lead me out of the study and down the hall, wondering along the way what the hell I was getting myself into.

I stopped cold when I saw the dining room, the white-table cloth laid out topped with silverware glowing in the light from several tapered candles. The situation had "romance" written all over it.

Jackson gestured me toward a chair and pulled it out for me. I hesitated, my knees bent, wondering what the procedure was here —should I start sitting or grab the bottom of the chair and pull it in?—but before I could feel too awkward, the cushion bumped the backs of my legs, and I sat as gracefully as possible.

This would definitely take some getting used to.

An older man bustled into the room and filled our glasses with white wine before setting a tray of delicate hors d'ouevres before us. He disappeared through the doorway as quickly as he came, giving me a deep bow on his way out. I stared across the table at Jackson, not sure what to say.

I felt like an explorer on an alien planet.

There are strange artifacts on this table, the likes of which are unseen on planet Earth. This mysterious contraption for example… Is it a torture device, or an implement for procuring sustenance?

Jackson saw me glaring down at the silverware.

"It's a shrimp fork," he said, leaning back with a smile.

"Oh. Good to know."

I felt myself blushing. What must I look like to him? Probably like something the cat dragged in from the back alley.

"I suppose you're wondering about the candles."

I chugged some wine and looked up at him. "Yep. Sure was. I thought you said you were going to keep it professional."

His eyes twinkled at me, his lips quirked into a half-smile.

"I also said the servants might talk. If you agree to take the job, my staff will already think you and I are dating. After all, I am having you over for a romantic dinner after meeting you at the youth center, remember?"

"Right," I said, staring down at the bone white plate before me. "You've got it all figured out."

"I don't like loose ends."

I looked up into Jackson's eyes, for a moment, looking past his handsome face and trying to read what was behind his seemingly perfect exterior. What was it like to live every moment under such scrutiny? To have to hide who you are in exchange for all this comfort? All that power, to meet his dreams with ease? Despite all his money, and all his luxurious possessions, he didn't have the freedom to relax. To be himself. To drop the image for one second and just be… free.

In a way, it was sad.

Jackson stared back at me, and suddenly, I wondered if he was reading me the same way. I didn't have money. Hell, I didn't have a dream to sell my freedom for. But with the money he offered for this job, I could have both. The dream and the freedom. And all in exchange for one year under the same scrutiny he faced every day.

"How do you do it?"

"What do you mean, Rose?"

"How do you live under all these prying eyes? Do you ever feel... I don't know. Trapped?"

He took a sip of his wine, assessing me with those eyes of his, so dark they were almost hypnotic.

"I don't really think about it. I grew up wealthy because of my father's auto empire, so I've always been under scrutiny," he said. "When I was younger, I played it fast and loose with my reputation, did what I wanted... But now, I've grown up. I know the price of such foolishness."

I nodded, thinking about his current dilemma. Living the way he wanted is why rumors were flying now, when he needed to be picture perfect for the campaign.

"But if you gave up the... you know..." I blushed again, and hated myself for being so shy about a subject so common as sex. "How do you...? Are you...?"

"Are you trying to ask if I'm happy with my love life?"

He smiled at me, but it didn't meet his eyes. Suddenly, I wished I was anywhere else but across the table from this man. What was wrong with me? Why did I always say the wrong thing?

"I didn't mean-"

"It's okay, Rose."

He cocked his head, assessing me again with his intense gaze.

"To put it simply, a personal life is a luxury I simply can't afford. Not when there's important work to be done."

I met his gaze, but I frowned, my lips pursing as I thought about that statement. He really did believe in what he was running for. But how could he give up so much to achieve his goals? Was he just driven, or was he just... cold? Maybe love didn't matter to men like Jackson Pierce. Or sex. Or companionship. Maybe all that mattered was work.

The thought made me shiver in my seat.

Then again, if he really meant what he said he stood for in his campaign, he and I were a lot alike. He wanted to fight for education reform and fund programs like my center to give kids and equal chance to succeed, no matter how humble their beginnings; how difficult their circumstances. Wasn't it worth giving up a social life for work like that?

"I'll help you," I said.

The words tumbled out of my mouth before I could think about them, surprising the both of us.

"I'll be your fake wife."

He smiled at me, but it didn't reach his eyes. Had I touched a nerve? He said he'd be blunt, so why could I?

"Excellent. Thank you, Rose."

The older man returned, carrying steaming bowls of soup on a silver tray. I stared down at my appetizer. I'd barely touched it, but it was whisked away before I could protest. He bowed and left us again, and I wondered what would happen to the leftovers. Did the staff get a crack at them? I hoped so. It would be a shame to waste such beautiful food.

"If you'll meet me at this location tomorrow," He said, handing me a business card with a hand-written address on it, "I'll have a contract drawn up guaranteeing payment after one year of service and outlining the details of the agreement. Can you come by at 2:00 p.m.?"

"My job might not let me get away."

"Rose," he said with a smirk. "What's your current salary?"

I raised an eyebrow.

"$28,000 a year."

Why lie?

"So you won't risk a long lunch at that job in order to secure a job paying five million?"

He grinned at me.

"Good point. I'll see you there."

He raised a glass to me, and we toasted, the mischievous glint in his eyes making me tingle all over.

"You won't regret it."

We drank deeply, and I wondered if he was right. Because despite the money, I was already starting to worry about what lay ahead. I had to remember who I was doing this for, and it would all be okay.

I just needed to stay focused.

CHAPTER 7

Mr. Pierce's lawyer pushed his glasses up his nose, practically scowling at my soon-to-be-boss.

"It's borderline fraud, for one, but as your constituents won't suffer a loss if they find out the truth, so it's unlikely anyone could successfully sue."

He sighed, shaking his head as he looked over the documents before him.

"I don't suppose I could stop you from going through with it?"

"I've made up my mind, Ken," Jackson said. "Thank you for drawing up the papers. Rose, if you would?"

I took the packet Mr. Pierce handed me and glanced down at the first page. The contract was surprisingly short, the terms clearly laid out, but not overwritten.

"It's all here?"

He sat across the table from me, the lawyer pacing in front of the wide, open windows overlooking the city. Jackson's short hair was tousled, as if he'd run his hands through it nervously, wondering if I'd show.

"Every detail. I asked Kenneth to make sure your protection is key in every aspect. You've already signed a confidentiality agreement, so now your comfort is paramount."

I looked down at the papers, a smile on my lips as I took in his words. For a politician, he wasn't the snake I'd expected.

Or maybe he was just a great salesman, and I was being naïve.

I started reading, pouring over the details. I wished I could hire a lawyer of my own to review the terms, but the cheapest I could find when I looked online was $250/hour. Seeing as I had $50 to my name until the next payday, that was definitely a no-go. Ironic that I had to take the job offer in order to afford the lawyer to look over the job's contract. Touché, Jackson.

Such is life in the real world, though. What are you gonna do about it?

There was nothing I could do except take a leap of faith.

I flipped through the pages, skimming as Jackson watched with bated breath. At the last page, I signed and dated, then pushed the papers back to him. It was done.

"Any questions?"

"When do we start?"

"I have a dinner to go to tomorrow night at the Empress Plaza. It would be a great place to make our dating scenario public, although I will have to give a speech, so you may be a little bored."

My eyes widened as I thought of an event like that. Who all would be there? Would it be televised? God, I hoped not... but what if it was? What would I wear?

"Boredom is the least of my worries."

"Here's my credit card," he said. "I've already called ahead and put you on my account, so you can sign for whatever you'd like."

I stared at the shining, black credit card in his hand.

"In case you needed something new to wear," he said, grinning at me. "Go get whatever you need."

I didn't move, but instead chewed my lip, staring at the card. I felt guilty for even looking at it.

"Don't worry, Rose. It won't bite."

He pushed it toward me until I finally closed my fingers around it, feeling like I was having an out-of-body experience.

"I don't... I don't need..."

"It's okay," Jackson said. "It's black tie. I know not a lot of people have evening gowns just lying around. I wouldn't even own a tux if I wasn't forced to go to things like this."

"But—"

"Take it, Rose. Go have fun. You're used to giving, so I'm sure this makes you uncomfortable, but you've earned it."

I gaped at him. Was he reading my mind?

"Besides," he said, winking, "Me paying for all of your expenses is part of the contract you just signed. Think of it like a corporate expense account. Off you go."

I didn't mention that I'd never imagined ever having a corporate expense account, much less been given unlimited access to a card like his.

He gave me one last smile before carrying the contract over to the lawyer's desk, both of them speaking in quiet tones. I let myself out of the office, wondering where the fuck people bought evening gowns at the last minute in this city.

Rich 'R' Us?

I wandered out of the law offices, wondering what to do next.

First, I officially quit my job, then I spent a fruitless afternoon driving around the outlet mall area, panic growing inside of me like a tumor. I wished for the first time in my life that I had a smart phone. Maybe there were boutiques somewhere in the city I just didn't know about, but damned if I even knew where to start searching.

Evening fell along with my gas barometer, and tears prickled behind my eyes. I swore and turned the car toward the one place I knew I could go for help, although it made me feel like a fool to do so.

I pulled into Jackson's campaign headquarters and took a deep breath. This was going to suck. One day on the job, and I'd already screwed things up. I'm sure he wouldn't be thrilled that I already needed his help, especially with something so simple he probably took it for granted. Or hired someone to shop for him, more likely.

I waffled in the entrance, the ringing of telephones and the hum of volunteer chatter filling my ears. I chewed my lip, wondering if I really wanted to bug him so soon, but unable to figure out what else to do. A middle-aged woman in an expensive-looking suit eyed me from across the room, then made a bee-line for me, smiling as she approached.

She stuck out her hand, red, lacquered nails gleaming under the fluorescent light.

"You must be Rose. I'm Lisa Stoneworth, Jacks's campaign advisor."

I shook her hand numbly, wondering how she could tell who I was. Was it really that obvious that I didn't belong, even here?

"Pleasure to meet you," I mumbled. "Is...um... Is Jackson available?"

Her eyes narrowed behind her glasses, and for a moment, she seemed to look right through me, into my soul. She tapped her lip with one finger, then nodded, like she knew exactly what I was up to.

"Come with me."

She took my arm, dragging me off the main floor and into a side office. I followed along without protest, glad to be out from the sea of gazes flicking curiously my way. She closed the door and whirled around, smiling at me like I'd just said something funny.

"Let me guess, sweetie," she said. "You need to doll up for tomorrow's dinner, but have no idea where to start."

I looked down at my sneakers, wincing as I noticed the duct tape holding the toe together on the left shoe.

"How did you know?"

"Listen, you sound like a good kid from what Jackson's told me, and I want to see him succeed. If you need help to make that success happen, I'm here to get the job done, no problem. It's what I do. Now, are you ready to listen to your new pal, Lisa? Cause I've got a list for you, and I want you paying attention."

Her words came out rapid-fire, and I stared like a deer in the headlights.

"Yes," I squeaked.

"Great, grab a pad of paper."

I looked around and snatched one off the shabby desk along with a chewed-looking pen.

"I've got some friends downtown who specialize in image prep, alright? Jacks has no head for this kind of stuff, so this is what I do. Now, listen. Go to Madeline's, address 2504 Grand Avenue, okay? Ask for Madeline by name and tell her Lisa sent you. She'll give you the full treatment, then, go to Ava, the spa on 34th Street, and tell them the same thing. They'll work you over."

I nodded, my stomach tying itself in knots as I scribbled her instructions, trying my hardest to keep up. After the salon, there was a meeting with a table etiquette coach tomorrow morning and a quick lesson on poise with another expert after that. By the time Lisa was done talking, I was already exhausted, thinking about the to do's before tomorrow night.

"Good luck, kid. Follow my lead, and you'll be great."

I thanked her quickly, and she winked at me over her glasses.

"And remember, only you, me, and Jackson are in on this little deal, so mum's the word with anyone else. Capisce?"

Her shrewd stare was starting to make me uncomfortable.

"Yep. Got it. No problem."

I pasted on a smile and escaped from the headquarters, hopping back into my little car and hitting the gas.

I headed to the first place on Lisa's list: a boutique called Madeline's. When I arrived, my mouth dropped open at the dresses in the window. They looked like something the first lady would wear, or something a beauty queen had hanging in her closet, sparkling and elegantly feminine. I swallowed hard, wondering if I still had time to flee the scene and just go in my slacks.

I saw Jackson's face in my mind's eye, his smile as he looked at me, trusting me not to blow this for the both of us.

I couldn't let him down, even if he had no idea how awkward something like this was for me. He didn't know how weird his life was. That much was obvious. As much as he tried to understand the rest of us, he was practically from another dimension.

I took a deep breath, and stepped out of the car, telling myself it would all be over soon. Nothing to worry about. It's just a dress, not a coffin full of spiders. Suck it up.

When I pushed open the door to the boutique, an elegant woman with short, silver hair cut in a bob smiled from behind the counter.

"May I help you?"

"Um…"

Her brow furrowed, her smile faltering. I took it she didn't like stuttering. My mouth went dry.

"Uh, Lisa sent me… Ma'am."

At the mention of Lisa's name, her face lit up again. She raised an eyebrow, assessing me from head to toe, a half smile playing on her burgundy lips.

"Well, then, my dear, you and I are going to have fun tonight. What's your name?"

"Rose," I croaked.

She crossed the room and took my hand, looking at me like I was a puzzle she couldn't wait to solve.

"You're a beautiful young woman, Rose, but you're not doing yourself any favors with these horrible clothes. What's the occasion we're shopping for, hmm?"

I furrowed my brow. I always dressed like this, casual, sure, but it was as nice as I could afford. Back off, lady.

"A dinner tomorrow night. A political one. Black tie."

"Ah, yes," she said, smiling at me. "No problem at all. Come with me, won't you?"

She swept off, gesturing for me to follow, her fingers glittering with rings.

"Mm, yes. You're a tall one. Thin. And these arms… hmm."

She prodded my muscles thoughtfully. It took everything I had not to cringe away.

"Well, let's see if we can't bring out that natural beauty with something… like…"

She pawed through the dresses, black silk and gleaming colored chiffon whirling as she moved.

"This."

My eyes widened as I took in the dress. I shook my head. It raised all the red flags: Strapless, armless, backless. Shameless.

"I can't."

Madeline smiled. "My dear, you can, and you will."

She grabbed my arm and dragged me into the dressing room, snapping the curtain shut behind us.

CHAPTER 8

When Jackson Pierce's car pulled up in front of my apartment, I was staring out the curtains, wishing I could call this whole thing off. Was the money worth the humiliation? Was it worth it if the cost was my dignity?

I patted my hair, swept to one side beneath my ear in a wave, like some kind of 1920s dancer. I glanced once in the mirror, checking my teeth for lipstick, and took a deep breath.

Here goes nothing.

I forced myself out of the apartment, down the stairs, and put one foot in front of the other until the driver opened the door, and I knew there was no going back.

When I ducked into the car, Jackson's face greeted me. He held his hand out, and I took it, letting him help me inside as I held my dress. The driver shut the door behind me with a nod and a small smile as he glanced at our hands entwined. The scent of Jackson's cologne met my nose, and I shivered, feeling his touch on my skin like a spreading warmth, making my whole body tingle.

"You look beautiful tonight," he said.

His eyes moved over me, shining with approval. I felt the heat creeping up my neck, and fought the urge to cover my cleavage, bared in the sweetheart neckline of the gown. I felt like I was overdoing it in the striking midnight blue fabric, shimmering softly as it hugged my curves, letting out below the knees. It took

Madeline a full half hour to talk me into it, but once I was in, I couldn't believe the reflection was me. I had to admit, I looked like a movie star compared to my usual jeans-and-tee attire.

I cleared my throat. "You're not so bad yourself."

He chuckled, but I wasn't joking. His hair stuck up in a sexy mess yet again, but he was more drool-worthy than usual in a crisp, black tuxedo, cufflinks gleaming at his wrists. Suddenly, I felt like a bond girl, riding beside a man with a license to kill, someone you didn't mess with unless you were looking for trouble. His energy as his eyes met mine was masculine, powerful. Sensual.

For the first time, I wondered what it would be like to be with him... What he'd look like wearing nothing but that bow-tie and a smile.

His thumb ran over my hand, and I let out a shallow breath, the sensation electric. I didn't realize we were still holding hands, and now I felt embarrassed, but I still couldn't bring myself to pull away.

As if reading my mind, he raised my hand to his lips, kissing my skin slowly, his lips unbearably soft and hot, his presence filling my every sense. I whimpered.

He leaned in, and I leaned to meet him, my mind screaming at me to stop, to not kiss this man I barely knew, the man hiring me to lie for him, to regain control before I did something truly stupid. But then, he turned his head, his lips brushing over my ear.

"Sorry to be so forward, but the driver needs to believe we're together..."

Reality crashed over me like a tidal wave.

"Of course," I whispered back.

He nuzzled my neck, and I let out a high-pitched, strained giggle, trying to play the part, shame filling me up from head to toe. How could I be so stupid?

I don't know what I'd expected when he spelled out the terms of the deal, but the way I reacted to his touch wasn't on the list. An uncomfortable mixture of embarrassment, arousal sloshed around inside of me like a chemical reaction gone wrong. I fixed a smile on my face and pulled away, although I left my hand in his. His eyes flicked upward to mine, and a little wrinkle formed above the bridge of his nose.

He stroked my hand again and looked away, out the window, into the darkness, and the cityscape passing us by.

I wondered if he'd felt my discomfort. Had I embarrassed him, too? I mean, he had to know this was strange, right? Playing with emotions, faking love? He had to know how difficult this would be, even if I hadn't fully understood, myself… right?

After all, he was the politician. He had to know what people thought and felt before they did, so he could persuade them to join his cause, to support him instead of the other guy. To change their hearts and minds. To call them to action. How could you do that without understanding emotions better than your average Joe, or in this case, Rose?

He had to know. He just had to. I refused to worry about his discomfort. It was pointless, when I had my own to worry about.

After all, I had to make this look right, and all while remembering which fork was which and trying not to let a boob fall out of this crazy dress. No pressure, or anything. I had to worry about me.

I followed his lead and stared out the window wondering how long dinner was going to take.

"Jackson, you son of a bitch!"

A man with quivering jowls grinned and slapped Jackson hard on the back.

"Glad you could come, young man! And when were you going to introduce me to this gorgeous thing you've been keeping to yourself all night, eh? I'm not going to live forever, you know!"

"Senator," he said, shaking the man's meaty hand. "Thank you for inviting me to speak tonight."

The man hand waved in Jackson's face and looked me up and down, his beady eyes scanning my body. I suppressed the instinct to kick him in the balls.

"This beautiful women accompanying me is Rose Turner," he said. "She's heavily involved in work with the local youth center. She-"

"Yes, yes," Senator Creep-sack said. "A pleasure my dear…"

His gaze turned greedy, and he grinned, a mouthful of yellowing teeth making my stomach turn. He grabbed my hand and lowered his quivering lips toward my skin. I winced, but Jackson pulled me out of harm's way just before I could get the full treatment.

God bless him.

"Now, Senator. One kiss from you, and I won't be able to hold onto her much longer! Your reputation with the ladies proceeds you."

He laughed, his grin utterly disarming. The fat man glared at Jackson for the space of a heartbeat, then roared with laughter, slapping him on the back again, so hard, I thought I heard his teeth rattle. Jackson's smile didn't falter.

"Have her all to yourself then, you boy scout bastard," he said. "Watch yourself around this one, young lady. He's slippery like the devil!"

I smiled, glancing sideways at Jackson. He really was, wasn't he.

"Thanks for the advice."

Shaking his head, the Senator moved on, yelling a greeting at another pair.

Jackson turned to me, his smile fading rapidly.

"I'm really sorry about him. He's… Senator Kelly is known for getting a little too friendly at these things. Especially when there's an open bar."

I glanced at the senator with a fixed expression, and tried not to wipe my hand on my gown. People were watching, eying the pair of us like we were the new Brangelina.

"I'm just glad he didn't slime me."

Jackson raised an eyebrow.

"You know, because of his… you know. Like Slimer."

He shook his head.

Wow, this joke did not land at all. Awkward.

"From Ghostbusters?"

He chuckled and offered a shrug.

"You've seriously never seen Ghostbusters? Did you grow up under a rock?"

This was too much. Was he Amish or something?

"My parents were very strict. Dad especially didn't approve of what he called 'time wasters,' including any kind of fantasy movies. If it wasn't something he thought was educational, I couldn't watch it."

"Wow. He sounds like a laugh riot."

Jackson gave me a half smile, looking at me carefully in that way of his, like I was a funny little puzzle, and he couldn't wait to figure me out.

"You have no idea," he said.

A silver-haired man in a tuxedo tapped a microphone onstage at the front of the banquet hall, hemming loudly to get everyone's notice. Wealthy donors and government officials turned their attention to him, although they still milled between elegantly decorated tables, the women's dresses sparkling like diamonds beneath the soft light of the chandelier.

"Thank you all so much for coming out. It's so wonderful to see all these friendly faces turning out to support our golden boy, Jacks Pierce."

The room echoed with applause.

"His father couldn't be here tonight, but in the spirit of this little gathering, I thought I'd share one of his favorite sayings with you all to start things off on the right foot. He used to ask me when I stopped by his office, 'Paul, do you know the difference between a shopping cart and a politician?' I said no, what's the difference, and do you know what he'd say?"

Jackson shifted on his feet, trying not to look at anyone in particular.

"A politician holds more liquor!"

Laughter mingled with groans. I elbowed him, smirking. Laugh riot indeed. He gave me a tight-lipped smile.

"On that note, enjoy the bar here and find your place cards. Dinner will be served shortly, followed by our honored guest speaker."

The group applauded again, people whispering and staring at Jacks and I with knowing smiles. Whenever I'd been the source of gossip growing up, it had always ended in a fist fight. I set my jaw and tried to breath, feeling like a fish out of water.

This was all normal. This is what we wanted—to get people talking. And then help them forget last week's rumors altogether. No punching necessary.

Jackson smiled and took my hand, his eyes taking in my stiff shoulders and tight jaw.

"Maybe I'd better get you a drink."

"Maybe you'd better make it a double."

He laughed and led me across the hall, his hand over mine, making me feel safe, anchored to him. After all, he dealt with these kind of people every day. With him, there was nothing to fear.

Or so I hoped, as we walked together, arm in arm, through a sea of staring faces.

As I sipped my drink, something strong involving a martini glass and a lemon twist, I tried to blend in with the two couples at our table. One couple was in their mid-fifties, and the other an even older man and a woman who I first thought was his granddaughter, but who he introduced as his wife.

I smiled hard and shook their hands, introducing myself as "a friend of Jackson's." The older couple shared sly glances, then smiled warmly at me. The younger woman gave me a cool look over her fake lashes and snuggled closer to her husband.

Jackson was shuffling index cards at the podium up front when the main course arrived, a delicious beef dish with some kind of red wine sauce. I'd never had anything like it, but after one bite, I was in carnivore heaven.

I groaned over a forkful.

The older woman shook her head, her lips pursed, apparently taking my groan for a critique.

"I know. I expect more for $1000 a plate. Last year there was a much higher standard. I mean, what is this, a bistro?"

She tittered, looking around the table. Her husband chortled beside her.

"You said it, dear."

Anger bubbled up inside me before I could tamp it back down and seal my yap.

"The kids I serve at the center get one hot meal per day, if they're lucky. One. And if I'm not mistaken, this event directly funds the campaign of a man who is working to change that. So let's enjoy what we've got, okay? Because from where I'm sitting, I feel pretty goddamn lucky to be eating at all."

I took another bite and mmm'd loudly enough for people at the next table to hear. They glanced over at us and frowned.

I pointed at the older woman's roll. "Are you going to eat that?"

She gawked at me, her hand caressing her pearls protectively. I gestured at it again with my butter knife and raised my eyebrows.

"N-no," she said. "You go right ahead, dear."

"Thanks so much."

I beamed at her and snatched the roll, making a show of buttering it, relishing it like it was a piece of birthday cake. I was soaking up some of the sauce with the rest of it when I heard Jackson's voice filling the hall.

"Good evening. I can't tell you how much your presence here tonight means to me. Together, we're going to do incredible things —things that wouldn't be possible without your generosity and your selfless support."

I smiled down at my plate as he continued. Selfless wasn't exactly the word I'd use, at least for the folks at my table.

Jackson outlined his philosophy and his goals for the campaign, touching on education and the lack of funding for local programs that aided so many children whose struggles would otherwise go unnoticed.

My heart swelled, listening to him, and my discomfort being here quickly melted away, replaced by a growing pride. I was proud to be his date tonight. Proud to be helping him. Proud that even among this crowd, this sea of privilege and power, he wasn't disappointing me. Maybe he really was the man he claimed to be. And just maybe, with enough donors like Grandpa Moneybags and Malibu Barbie, he could make a real difference.

I watched him, so graceful and confident, even in front of a huge crowd, smiling when he drew a laugh, and sighing when he lowered his voice and everyone seemed to lean in, hanging on his every word.

As weird as this situation was, being here with him, supporting him, admiring him, felt right. I smiled as I polished off the rest of my steak, feeling better about this arrangement than I had since Jackson Pierce came into my life.

When he was done, I applauded loudly with the rest, and when the couples looked back at me, congratulating me on his behalf, I took the rest of the rolls and slid them delicately into my purse, watching their eyes as they struggled not to say anything offensive.

What can I say? Sometimes a girl just wants to have fun.

CHAPTER 9

He opened the car door, and I collapsed inside, laughing as I pulled my skirt down where it was supposed to be.

"I think I had one too many cocktails in there," I said.

Jacks slid in next to me and exhaled hard. He chuckled low in this throat, grinning at me as I leaned back against the headrest.

"I think you had the right idea. I could have used a martini or three talking with those folks all night long. I thought I'd never escape. Thank God the dancing started, and I had an excuse to break free."

I smiled, remembering the way he'd leaned over the table, extending his hand to me, his dark eyes mesmerizing even in the sea of twinkling candles and dazzling luxury surrounding us. When he asked me to dance, I didn't know what to say, but one reassuring wink from him was all it took to bring me to my feet, my hand sliding into his. His touch was electric as he led me to the floor.

I thought I'd be embarrassed dancing in front of all these curious eyes, but when his hand touched the small of my back and he pulled me close everything else faded away. We floated in a sea of darkness, the ballroom all to ourselves, everyone else just a distant memory. He smiled down at me, his face so close to mine I could press my cheek to his if I dared.

He leaned in and whispered in my ear.

"You're doing great."

I bit my lip and let him hold me close, swiveling me effortlessly as he led, guiding me in the steps as we swayed together, his body warm against mine, his rough palm against my skin making me shiver.

"Thank you for coming to my rescue," he said.

Now, driving back in his car, he linked his hand in mine against the leather seat. I was dizzy, intoxicated by his presence, the musky scent of his cologne, and the way he looked at me as if this was more than just a business deal. As if I was his woman tonight., and he wanted me. And what was more, I felt the connection, the spark between us. I knew I shouldn't think like that, but at the moment, I didn't care.

I felt reckless. Maybe for once in my life, I could just relax and enjoy the ride, instead of worrying about getting hurt.

"Any time," I said.

Jackson pressed a button, and the partition between us and the driver rolled up, but not before I saw the driver wink at him in the rearview mirror.

What a snoop. I smiled, feeling the blush creep onto my cheeks. What must he think of us?

"So," he said. "What do you want to do now?"

He still held my hand, stroking it softly with his thumb in a way that made my sex ache and my heartbeat pound in my throat.

"It would make sense for you to come back to my place, even if you don't stay for the night," he offered.

"Mm," I said, looking down at his hand, wondering what it would feel like running over other parts of my body.

"Unless, of course, you have other plans. Or… aren't comfortable with that."

"I'm comfortable," I said. "I mean, I'll come over. If you want."

"Perfect."

He grinned, his smile less-than-innocent, or was that just my imagination?

"I was hoping you'd say that. I have to admit, Rose… I don't want the night to end just yet. You're great company."

I turned back to my window, smiling, wondering what he meant by that. Was I a friend, or was he feeling the electricity, too? We drove in silence the rest of the way, his hand never leaving mine.

* * *

One glass of wine later, we sat comfortably in Jackson's living room on a sectional sofa big enough for three to sleep on, a projector screen lowered and ready to rock.

"So, you really haven't seen Ghostbusters?"

"I really haven't."

"That, Mr. Pierce, is a child abuse. We need to make up for lost time and educate you about one of the best movies ever made. I mean, Citizen Kane, move over. It's that good."

He raised an eyebrow, and I cracked up, watching his expression.

"I'm ordering it right now," he said, picking up his universal remote. "But, if I don't like it, you'll have to pay a price."

I sipped my wine, intrigued. "Oh?"

"How about this." He grinned mischievously. "If I'm not loving it after a half hour, you have to tell me anything I want to know about you, even if it's one of your deepest secrets."

"Like truth or dare?"

He took a swig of his wine and topped us off from the bottle of Pinot Gris.

"But more mature, of course." He winked at me and laughed.

"Of course," I said. "Okay, fine, but if you do like it, I get to grill you instead. How do you like them apples?"

"Deal."

"Besides," I said. "If you don't like it you're probably dead inside, and that's all I need to know about you."

He shook his head, a half smile on his face. I was sure he wasn't used to people messing with him, considering he was always surrounded by servants and campaign staff. A little light ribbing was probably good for him. Built character.

"Fair enough."

I scooted back on the couch, tugging down my skirt again. This damn dress kept riding up, that is, when it wasn't riding down in other areas.

"Would you like to borrow something more comfortable to wear? It's no problem."

I grinned, wondering if he had a closet of women's clothing somewhere. Is this why he needs a fake wife? Is he J. Edgar Hoover, Jr.?

"That would be great. I didn't want to say anything, but this dress is working my last nerve."

"Come on, then."

He helped me up, my hands in his, and I felt that little jolt again at his touch. He led me down a narrow hallway and up to the third level of the house. When he pushed the last door open, my eyes widened. A gigantic master suite opened up before me, a four-poster canopy bed sitting up a level across from the biggest walk-in closet I'd ever seen. I think it was actually bigger than the bedroom in my apartment, and filled to the brim with suits, slacks, and rows of polished dress shoes.

Was this his bedroom? One word: Wow.

"I've got some t-shirts and things in the drawers on the right. I'll leave you alone so you can make yourself comfortable. Borrow anything at all—I really don't mind." He smiled, his dark eyes crinkling at the corners. "Can you find your way back to the living room?"

"I think so," I said. "But you might want to leave a trail of breadcrumbs just in case."

He chuckled low in his throat, his eyes wandering over me slowly, like he was taking one last look at me in my slinky dress. I smoothed it down, suddenly feeling shy.

"Don't take too long, or I might change my mind about this ghost-blaster movie," he said.

He turned and shut the door, and I shook my head. It was too weird being in the bedroom of such a powerful man, but the weirdest thing of all was that it felt natural being with him, even in his almost-castle. He had a way of making me feel cared for, like he not only enjoyed my company but cared about my happiness. That was rare for me, and definitely didn't go unnoticed.

I wasn't comfortable around a lot of people. Not since I was a kid and saw how cruel they could be. How cold. But something about Jackson Pierce made me feel like maybe, just once, I could let my guard down. It was a good feeling.

I slipped carefully out of the gown, and hung it up at the front of the closet, next to a row of Armani suits, not wanting to ruin something so fine by tossing it on the floor. Then, I slid out of the strapless bra that had been pinching me all night, wishing I brought my regular one, but deciding not to sweat it. I wasn't exactly Dolly Parton in that area, after all. It would probably be fine to go without.

I found a well-worn AC/DC t-shirt in the drawer and goggled at it, then laughed as I slipped it over my head.

Really?

It was hard to imagine someone so straight-laced rocking out at an AC/DC concert, but the evidence was right in front of me. Jackson Pierce was just full of surprises. I wondered what else I didn't know about him. What surprises he had in store beneath that polished exterior.

I searched through the drawers until I found a pair of silk boxers that looked too good to resist. I wondered if he'd mind, but then remembered his words and pulled them on.

It was so intimate, wearing these things of his. But the feel of the soft, threadbare cotton and silk against my skin made me bold. I padded barefoot back down the stairs, through the hallway and pushed open the door to the entertainment room.

Jacks looked up from a fresh bowl of popcorn.

"I've got it all cued up. I hope you like pop…"

His voice faded away, his eyes widening as he took me in, moving over my braless breasts, barely visible in the draped shirt, and down to my bare legs beneath his boxer shorts.

"I hope this is okay," I said.

"Yeah… No problem."

I plopped down on the sofa beside him, noticing he'd managed to change into some pinstriped pajama pants and a crisp, white tee. I wondered if he had a spare set in this closet so he didn't have to make the trip to his room every time he wanted to kick back and veg out. The thought made me smile, considering he literally had a butler to get him whatever he wanted. Just like him to be so self-sufficient, even with his lavish lifestyle.

I leaned over and grabbed a handful of popcorn, and he leaned back against the sofa, letting out a deep breath as my thigh grazed his. I glanced over, and his back was stiff, his hands flat on his thighs. He looked like he was willing himself to relax.

Was he nervous? Why would he be nervous about watching a movie?

If anyone should be nervous, it was me, sitting here next to this intriguing, gorgeous man, the feel of his thigh on mine all I could think about as he settled in and turned on the projector.

CHAPTER 10

I tried not to stare as Rose sat next to me, her thigh so close to mine, her bare skin glowing in the dim light from the television. The idea of her sweet body caressing the inside of the boxers I slept in was almost too much to cope with. I pulled a pillow onto my lap, pretending I needed it to balance the popcorn bowl, hiding the erection now tenting my pajama bottoms.

She leaned back on the couch, the cushions shifting, bringing her closer to me as the down settled. Her leg grazed mine, but she didn't pull away. She grew still, and I wondered if she could feel it, too. The heat between us… If she felt the effect she had on me, sitting so close, wearing so little, her breasts bare beneath the thin cotton of my old t-shirt.

I turned to the screen, watching but not really seeing as Bill Murray snuck through a library, proton pack at the ready. Rose made a small sound beside me, and I saw her smile as he and Dan Akroyd approached a ghostly librarian. My eyes traced her mouth, those full lips curving delicately, her eyes outlined with lush, dark lashes, her short hair messily tucked behind one ear, already falling out of its slick, formal style.

What would it be like to kiss her? To pull her onto my lap, to knock the popcorn to the carpet, forgotten, and make her shudder in my arms? Would she protest? Or would she kiss me back? Grind against me, loving how hard she made me just by her presence beside me?

The ghost rushed toward the screen, and Rose screeched happily beside me as the two men yelled in terror. I smiled then, watching her, wondering what her childhood was like—what she was like the first time she saw this movie. There was so much I didn't know about her. So much I longed to understand.

She glanced over at me and grinned, giving me a playful shove with her elbow.

"You're not watching at all! Already bored?"

"No, not at all."

I focused on the screen, and struggled to watch, enjoying the movie, even though 90% of my attention was on that soft, smooth thigh pressing against mine, the heat of her body a delicious distraction.

After a while, she leaned against me, but I wasn't sure if she was engrossed in the film, falling asleep, or if, like me, she was inwardly holding her breath, caught up in the tension between us, wondering what might happen on a night like this.

After a half hour, I paused the movie.

She glanced up at me, her cheek resting on my shoulder.

"So? What do you think?"

"I'm really enjoying myself," I said, truthfully. "And if I recall correctly, that means you get to ask me whatever you want."

She propped herself up on her elbow and smiled, dazzling me with the sincerity of the expression, the easy way she showed her emotions. It was disarming, her vulnerability utterly beautiful.

"Ha! I knew you'd love it. Okay… what to ask…"

She lay her head on her arm, gazing at me, her long neck graceful, even more elegant juxtaposed against my ratty old t-shirt.

"What did you want to be when you grew up, Jackson? Did you think you'd be here? Running for Governor?"

"That's three questions," I said.

She frowned, and I laughed.

"But since I'm such a good guy, I'll answer them all."

I poured the last of the wine, and handed her a glass. I sipped as I thought of the best way to respond. No one had ever asked me that. Maybe no one would dare, just in case the answer was something other than 'I'm right where I want to be.' I looked at Rose, watched her watching me. This woman was fearless.

I liked it.

"A firetruck."

She stared at me for a moment, then cracked up, her whole face lighting up in a way that made my cock stir beneath the pillow. God, this woman…

"You mean a firefighter? Or seriously the truck?"

"The truck. Of course," I said. "Why be a firefighter when you can be a big, shiny red truck. Just makes sense, really."

She giggled beside me, falling back against the couch, then drained the last of her wine from the glass.

"But, then I turned five, and my real ambition set in. After that, I only wanted to be one thing."

"What was that? A dump truck?"

"How dare you. That's ridiculous," I said. "I wanted to be Batman."

She stared at me in disbelief.

"Seriously?"

"Seriously. Still do."

"I wanted to be Batman, too."

Our thighs touched again as she settled into the cushions, pulling her legs up on the sofa. A jolt of awareness pulsed through me, her body so close, I could feel her heat.

"My mother bought me a Batman t-shirt from a thrift store… I mean, before she passed away. The other kids made fun of me, said it was a boys' shirt, but I didn't care."

Her eyes were serious now, deep pools that a man could lose himself in if he wasn't careful.

"I think Batman appealed to me because his billionaire playboy thing was the real illusion. The face he presented to society was the costume. Bruce Wayne was the mask, and when he put on the cowl and became Batman, he was finally himself. He could help people however he wanted, without fear. Without pressure to perform," I said.

"I think I get that."

"I think I also related to being raised by the butler."

I laughed, trying to make it sound like a joke, a throw-away, but it sounded as bitter as I felt, remembering those days of vying for my father's attention, my mother ignoring me, too busy with country club activities to remember to actually care for her sons.

"My father was a soldier," Rose said. "He was in Saudi Arabia for months during the Gulf War."

I raised my eyes to hers. She looked at me, and the sadness reflected in her eyes made my own pain fade away, forgotten.

"My mother got pregnant almost as soon as he got back, and I think it was just too much for him. She said he would wake up screaming in the night, that he couldn't drive because his anxiety was so bad… and the VA hospital had a backlog. They couldn't see him for over a year."

"What happened?"

Rose looked down at her hands, fidgeting in her lap. "He… he, um…"

"It's okay…"

I put my hand over hers, and she didn't pull away. She looked over at the popcorn, her eyes unfocused, and I could tell she was gazing into the past.

"He locked himself in the bathroom one night, shortly after I was born. By the time my mom found him, he was already dead. He used his razor… She wasn't the same after that. She got to a really bad place over the next couple of years and finally the state took me away. I remember visiting her off and on when I was three or four years old, but it's blurry. They tell me I was five when she finally OD'd."

I stroked her hand, my head spinning, feeling like an ass complaining about a family that was still breathing, despite their problems.

I'm a fucking idiot. I knew she was a foster child. Why bring up being raised by the butler? What must she think of me? Stop being so selfish, Jackson, and focus on someone else for a change...

"Jesus," I breathed.

"I wanted to be Batman because he was an orphan, you know? He didn't have anyone, he was alone, but he became a hero anyway. He didn't just... give up. I used to imagine that one day I could save people, protect people, instead of being the one who needed protecting."

"Rose... I didn't mean..."

She looked up at me, her eyes clear, dry and tearless. Strong and bold and haunted, but refusing to let her ghosts overcome her. Looking at her in that moment, made me feel strong as well.

Without thinking, I cupped her face with my hands and kissed her.

CHAPTER 11

When he kissed me, my world stopped turning. Time froze, and I lost myself, my worry, my sorrow, my doubt running off me like rainwater as his lips met mine, his hands wrapping in my hair, pulling me to him. He tasted like sweet wine, his mouth soft and hot and urgent, his chin dusted with new stubble, rough and masculine against my skin.

I parted my lips, my heart thudding in my chest, my mind a blank, all of my sadness flying away as quickly as it came, memories fleeting against the strength of this moment. Against the strength of his arms, holding me tight.

Popcorn tumbled to the floor as we came together, our bodies pressing close as he tugged me onto his lap, the throw pillow falling off to the side. I wrapped my arms around his neck, breathless, feeling like I was drowning in him, but refusing to come up for air. I dug my fingers into his short hair, nails scraping his scalp, loving the way our hearts beat together, our breathing now thick. Heavy.

He groaned and ran his tongue over my bottom lip, making me shiver.

I felt his arousal beneath me and gasped. A voice deep inside my mind whispered *This is wrong! You're going to get hurt, Rose!* but I couldn't stop the energy between us. And what's more, I didn't want to. I was swept away on a current of impulsivity, of lust and heat. And something more…

Jackson was like me.

He understood what so many couldn't. From the look on his face, I knew what he'd implied, but didn't have to say. He felt like as much of an orphan as I was. Even though he had everything money could buy, he didn't have what he wanted most. Someone who loved him unconditionally.

Pain and pleasure came together as we shared a breath, our kisses now desperate and rough. His teeth scraped my lip, and it was my turn to join my tongue with his, to taste him, to let myself explore him, his scent filling my nostrils, the feel of his mouth on mine more intoxicating than any wine.

He pressed me back onto the cushions and moved over me, his lips on my neck now, hot and wet, making me moan with each touch, each delicious sensation. He pressed his body between my thighs, his stiffness rubbing against me now, the cotton and silk between us feeling like nothing as his heat covered me. I wriggled beneath him, grinding against him, sighing wantonly as my core ached, pulsing with need, tingling with pleasure, the friction making me wild for him.

I wanted more.

I tugged on the bottom of his t-shirt, and he sat up, yanking it up over his head. He paused for a moment, panting, his dark eyes animalistic, hungry, almost frightening in the dim light. I'd never seen him like this, so out of control, and the sight of his gorgeous, muscular body, tanned and fit, made me want to give up my control as well. To release my fear and doubt and give myself fully to this moment with him.

Just for one night. Just for one night, I would do the wrong thing without second guessing myself. Without guilt. Without worry about what the future may hold.

Because it felt so damn right, I didn't think I could stop if I wanted to.

I pulled the oversized tee over my head, my hair in my face, and heard him suck in a harsh breath above me. I blew my bangs out of my eyes, and moaned when I saw the look on his face, his eyes hooded, his gaze crawling over me, as intense as any physical touch.

My nipples pebbled beneath that gaze, my small breasts upswept and begging to be covered by his strong hands.

When he lowered his mouth to me, I cried out beneath him. He kneaded one breast, his rough palm on my tender flesh making me squirm, and suckled on the other, cupping the bottom, lifting my nipple to his lips. His tongue darted out, flicking me, before he drew on me, making my back arch and my whole body tremble.

My hips bucked against him, our bodies meeting again, and he growled, lifting his head from one breast to the other. I gripped his hair hard, loving the way he suckled me, never wanting it to end, but at the same time wanting more... needing more. Needing all of him.

"Please," I gasped.

He looked up, his hands squeezing my breasts, covering me like I was made to fill his palms, and grinned like a jackal.

"You're so beautiful," he breathed. "So fucking beautiful, Rose..."

He slid his hands down my back until he cupped my ass. He pulled me up by the hips, grinding his hard-on against me, even as my shoulders lay back on the couch, my body arched, trusting him to hold me. I whimpered, letting him rub me over his cock, using me, making my toes curl with each stroke against his stiffness.

"Do you want this, Rose? Want me inside of that tight little body of yours?"

I moaned at his words. This was so unlike him, this ragged, sexual being above me. Where was the stiff politician? The boy scout? He was gone just like I was, lost to the heat between us, transformed into something else, something real.

"Yes..."

He slid the boxer shorts off my body, hooking my panties with them, and tossed them across the room. I was naked before him now, exposed, as his eyes moved lower. He ran his hands down my belly reverently, then over the insides of my thighs, driving me crazy with his touch.

"You want my rock hard cock in you, Rose?"

His fist knotted in my hair, and he brought his face so close to mine, I could feel his breath on my lips.

"You want me to fuck you harder than you've ever been fucked in your life?"

I gasped. A brief stab of fear melted into an animal lust as I saw the look in his eyes. His grip tightened, bending my neck back. I was so wet from his words, my arousal leaking onto my thighs.

"Yes," I breathed. "Please, Jackson…"

He grinned at my response, then bit my lip hard. He sucked it between his own, his tongue kissing away the sting.

He leaned back and undid his pajama bottoms, slipping them down along with his boxers. My eyes widened as I saw him, erect and totally mouth-watering; thick and gorgeous, and all for me.

He leaned forward, rubbing the fat tip of his cock against me, teasing my folds, making me whimper, my core hot and throbbing for him. He dipped a finger into me, and I panted, my mouth hanging open, watching him with widened eyes. His own gaze was locked on mine, watching me react as he teased me, pumping first one finger inside of me, then two, curling them upward inside of me in a "come hither" gesture. I bit my lip, all of it too much, but at the same time, not enough.

I reached for him, wanting to touch him, to stroke him, to urge him to hurry the hell up already, but he slapped the back of my hand, his eyes flashing dangerously.

"Don't you dare," he said through gritted teeth.

He reached forward and captured my wrists in his hands.

"You are mine. Mine. You don't touch me without my permission. Understood?"

I stared at him, my eyes watering, both from the surprise and the sting on the back of my hand. Who was this man?

"Yes," I breathed.

"Yes, what?"

He tightened his grip on my wrists, looming over me, the tip of his erection pressing into me.

What did he want from me? I hazarded a guess.

"Yes… Sir?"

He slammed into me, and I screamed, the shock of him inside of me mingling with a full feeling so delicious I almost came undone. Apparently, I'd guessed right.

"Good girl," he whispered in my ear, his rough beard scratching my cheek. "You feel incredible…"

I sighed, my body squeezing around him, loving the way he fit inside of me, thick almost to the point of pain, my body adjusting by increments as he pressed into me, waiting, his body stretched over me, his weight a comfort as he held me fast.

He began to move, then, his hand still capturing both my wrists above my head. I moaned as he pistoned inside of me, his strokes long and even, the friction making my whole body quake.

His lips came down on mine again, his tongue teasing mine, sucking, tasting, dancing, matching the rhythm of his hips. He kneaded my breast with his other hand, his palm on my nipple making my body tense around him. I wanted to hold him, to tease him like he was teasing me, to grab his ass and pull him closer, but I was captured. Totally at his mercy, his control, as he bucked into me.

I kissed him back, eager for him, my body moving to meet him with each stroke, my hips lifting, my thighs squeezing him with each sweet motion. I'd never been dominated like this, and now, even as my pleasure ramped up with each thrust, sparks flying through me like I was a live wire, exposed by him, I realized I trusted Jackson completely.

I trusted him not to hurt me, even as he frightened me, pinning me down and taking me like an animal, right there on his couch. I realized I felt free. Free to feel, free to enjoy, free to let him take me where he wanted me, to give me the pleasure we both craved, but without the responsibility of worry.

Free to just be his.

My hands clenched into fists as he picked up the pace, thrusting into me harder and harder, deeper and deeper, ramming into me like a man possessed. I cried out, my voice muffled against his lips, and I felt him grin against me. His hand moved from my breast, and he snuck it between us, thumbing my clit in a way that made me squeal, my body on fire for him, so hot I thought I might burn away, turning to ash beneath him.

"Cum for me," he said.

He gazed into my eyes, and I felt lost, helpless to disobey him as he stroked me, fucking me harder and harder, again and again.

"Cum now, my beautiful girl…"

I gasped, my wrists straining against him as my body responding, my orgasm crashing over me, my eyes locked on his, seeing my own pleasure reflected in them even as I came apart around him, convulsing from the inside out.

He held me tight, pumping inside of me again and again, until finally, he groaned, and I felt him twitching inside of me, spilling into me, his pleasure mixing with my own until I wasn't sure where I ended and Jackson began. I bucked upward, seeking him, and he pressed down, locking together with me, both of us riding wave after wave, our breath mingling as we shared the moment, face to face, kissing and gasping and watching one another.

Finally, he lay down on top of me, gathering me in his arms, and I wrapped my legs around his waist, enjoying the connection as our breathing quieted, our hearts beating together. After a long while, he pressed a kiss to my lips and smiled down at me, stroking my hair.

Neither one of us said a thing, but now that it was over, I couldn't help but wonder what it meant. Or did it have to mean anything?

"I have a spare bedroom made up," he said. "If you'd like to stay."

He slipped out of me and sat back on the couch. I felt his words like a slap. The spare room? Obviously, he didn't want me to stay in his bed, even after this. Maybe he was already regretting tonight. Already telling me where I stood. He'd only share the master suite when it was time for our fake marriage to begin, and not any sooner.

Well, Jackson. Message received.

"I should probably go…"

I thought about leaving, running away, and realized he'd have to rouse his driver at this late hour to take me. After all, I'd come home in his car, and besides, I had too much wine to drive, even if I'd met him here.

"Actually, the spare room sounds good," I said, sighing.

I gathered the boxers and t-shirt, my cheeks heating with embarrassment. What must he think of me? This is supposed to be a business arrangement, and here I am, naked in his living room. This was all my fault.

I should never have done something so stupid. So fucking reckless.

Jesus, Rose. What did you think would happen?

He led me down the hall and up the stairs, to a room adjacent to his own. He pointed out the washroom and gave me one last look, the emotion in his dark eyes inscrutable.

"Goodnight, Rose."

I pressed my lips together and nodded, closing the door behind me. It seemed there was nothing left to say, nothing to discuss about what we'd just shared.

I lay on bed, watching the starlight shift across the ceiling, and tried to let it go. Because for a moment, in his arms, I'd actually thought I was something special to him.

Give me a break. I was so naïve sometimes, I just made myself sick.

CHAPTER 12

I spent the next day in my apartment, cooking up a storm, trying to shut down my thoughts with hard work and a good sweat. It might have worked, too, if Jackson hadn't insisted I take his credit card to the store in order to "buy whatever I wanted for the kids." Even my work at the center was wrapped up in his business now. Him and his damn money.

Did this even count as generosity, since he had more than he could ever spend?

But since it was his buck, and since I wanted something to distract myself, I soon had three dutch ovens packed with beef short ribs going on the stove, and I paced back and forth, stirring and tasting, pouring my heart into my work, trying not to think, not to feel, at least for a little while.

Damn him. Damn him and his stupid, generous… No! Don't think. Just cook. Just focus on what's at hand, Rose, and you'll be alright.

But eventually, it was time to wait, time to stop lifting the lids and letting the steam escape, and all my thoughts came rushing back.

What was that last night? What was I thinking? I never slept with men so soon, and never a man I wasn't even dating. Okay, so I hadn't exactly had a lot of experience, and if I was honest with myself, it had been far too long since my last boyfriend a few years back. I was definitely rusty. But this just wasn't like me! Part of me worried I'd lost my mind.

And to make things worse, this was supposed to be business. Business. And business meant not getting involved, especially when the arrangement was this weird, this emotionally charged… this dangerous for both of our hearts and lives. We couldn't get tangled up. Not when this was all supposed to be over in a year, no harm, no foul.

But the part that really worried me, the part that was spinning around and around in my head, was the change that came over him as soon as he kissed me. The polite façade fell away, and what replaced it was so rough and aggressive… He frightened me, holding my wrists the way he did, commanding me. Controlling me.

Or did he?

I chewed my lip, staring at the pots on the stove, replaying the night. If I was honest with myself, the thing that scared me the most was how much I'd liked it. How hard I fell into a rhythm with him, how easily my body responded to his demands. I wanted him to take me, to use me. To make me his.

I hated that.

Flashes of memory came into my mind, unwanted.

An image of myself curled in the corner, the room impossibly big to my child's eyes, my first foster brother standing over me with a lamp cord in his hand, ready to whip me again, my arms already covered in angry, red welts.

My teddy bear, the one my father gave me before he died, in the mud, rain falling on it as I shivered, locked out of the house, the colorful flickering of the TV visible through the window, reflected on my caretaker's faces.

Mother, crumpled on the floor, the needle still in her arm as the pot on the stove boiled over.

No matter how much I thought I trusted this man, he was just going to hurt me. I had to be careful, be cautious. I had to protect myself. After all, no one would do it for me. Never had, never will.

Especially since I was the one putting myself in danger, letting this man get to me like this.

I ran my hands over my face and realized my cheeks were wet. I stood up, brushed myself off, and started chopping vegetables for cole slaw. At least I was control of this much, even if it was just dinner.

The knife rose and fell, the soothing sounds of the blade hitting wood taking me away to a safer place. A place where I was whole again and no one could make me cry.

CHAPTER 13

"She was a hit last night, Jacks."

Lisa blocked my doorway, her eyes shining behind her Gucci glasses.

"Everyone loved her. Well, okay, except for the couple at her table who said she was sanctimonious. But that's okay! Sanctimonious works for us. Your voters are holier-than-thou bleeding heart types. They'll eat her up."

I tried to focus on her words, but at that moment, all I could remember was the taste of Rose's skin, the way her sweet breasts fit in my hands as I kissed her, savoring the way she gave herself to me, the way her passion matched my own. I was still reeling from last night, still not quite believing it really happened.

She was so different than any women I'd ever been with.

Instead of the women I met at the club, women who advertised their love for submission, but continually tried to control me, topping from the bottom as I fought to please them, Rose was almost fragile, and I could tell the way she responded to me was completely genuine, completely unrehearsed. The look of surprise in her eyes when I took control, the heat reflected there as she succumbed to her desire, moved me like no one else ever had.

She was a natural. I couldn't stop thinking about her.

"So unless you do something foolish, I think we're going to pull this off."

I looked up, startled out of my thoughts.

"Foolish?"

"Yeah, I mean, we're looking good so far, so let's just keep the momentum going as we get this wedding planned. Don't do anything to scare her off."

Lisa winked at me and backed out of my office, shutting the door behind her.

Don't do anything to scare her off...

Her words made me pause, my mind going over everything I said before we made love, all that happened during, and everything after. What did Rose think about all this?

What if I'd just complicated things? What if things became strained between she and I after last night's intimacy? After all, what did this mean to the both of us? I hadn't had a relationship in years... Did I even want one?

Did she?

Maybe she thought last night was a mistake... Maybe I came on too strong. I needed to talk to her. Feel this out before it became an issue. The last thing I wanted was for my damage control to turn into another problem. My reputation simply couldn't handle it. I needed Rose on my side, being the perfect, respectable wife, and if she was pissed off or worried or...

I needed her comfortable with our arrangement much more than I needed the fleeting pleasure of a sexual relationship. Those never lasted long for me anyway, but the good I could do in office was long-term. That's what I needed to keep my focus on—what mattered. What would endure.

I leaned back in my chair and ran my hands over my face.

Complications always led to trouble. I needed to keep things simple between Rose and I, and that meant keeping it professional. It was the only thing that made sense. We needed to talk about dialing things back between us and going through with the original plan. We'd be seen together, we'd get married, and she'd move in. It would be for show, and that was that.

She'd understand. For all I knew, it might even be a relief. She was a practical woman, after all, and had a lot on her plate. She might be waiting to suggest the same thing…

So why did my chest ache when I thought about telling her?

I sighed and stared out at the campaign office, at the bustle of my interns and volunteers, the people who kept my campaign running and kept my hopes alive. I was doing this for them. For the voters. For my community and my state, to make things better for all of us.

I needed to remember that.

Matters of the heart didn't matter when it came to doing the right thing.

I turned back to my desk, and looked at my schedule for the day. Work was waiting for me. It was time to put childish things aside and focus on what was at stake.

CHAPTER 14

When I arrived at the youth center that night, Kathy met me at the curb, beaming from ear to ear as I unloaded my trays of food.

"He's ba-aaack!"

She giggled, her round cheeks rosier than usual. I raised an eyebrow and handed her a serving dish full of cheesy polenta.

"Who's back?"

"Your handsome politician, of course," she said, her voice high and breathy. "He's just like a Kennedy… If my Morty had a head of hair like that, I'd never let him leave the bedroom!"

I shook my head, sighing. Of course he was back. We had a deal after all—be seen together so the relationship looked real. He knew I'd be here, so here he was, ready to get down to business.

I was just a guest bedroom to him, after all. Just a little indiscretion on the road to getting reelected… I had to think of it that way, and not dwell on thoughts of last night. It would only lead to more trouble.

I flushed, thinking of the way he'd felt inside of me, and shook myself mentally. He wasn't here for that, and he never would be again. I knew that. Last night had been a mistake, a mixture of drinking and vulnerable topics and… and… whatever.

"So are you two, you know? Together?"

Kathy giggled again, and I frowned, hefting two more trays out of my trunk. I didn't want to encourage her, but I had agreed to this. I didn't have much of a choice.

"Yeah. We're seeing each other. It's all pretty new, but-"

I was cut off by a squeal of delight.

"You're so lucky! Oh, my Lord, Rose, I can't believe you were keeping him a secret! If he were my man, I'd be shouting it from the rooftops, let me tell you."

We walked through the back doors into the kitchen, and all I wanted to do was get to work setting up for dinner service.

"You hang onto this one, Rose." Kathy set down the tray and waggled a finger at me. "Don't do that thing you do."

"What thing is that?"

I was getting pissed off now, but I had kids to feed, so I couldn't let it get to me. I'd worked with Kathy long enough to know that if I didn't let her finish, she'd never leave me alone.

"You know very well, Rose," she said. "You push people away. You have to keep your heart open. Otherwise how is love ever going to get in?"

She nodded knowingly at me, looking like a mother hen.

I fought back the urge to tell her to fuck off.

"Mm hmm," I grunted. "Thanks, Kathy."

She beamed at me. "Any time."

Jackson Pierce pushed through the door, carrying a sponge and a bucket of water. He smiled when he saw me, but I noticed it didn't reach his eyes.

"I'll leave you two alone," Kathy said, winking. "Let you get ready for dinner without me in the way."

She giggled behind her hand one more time as she passed Jackson, and disappeared into the dining room.

I put down my trays and began organizing things, wishing I had more time to think of what to say to him. A large hand touched the small of my back, making me jump.

"Rose."

I kept my eyes on my work, trying not to think about the intoxicating scent of his cologne, of the heat of his body, so near I could lean back onto his chest. Get lost in him again.

"Rose, look at me."

I looked up and met his eyes, dark and alluring. A bolt of fear shot through me. What was he going to say? That last night was a mistake? Or that he wanted me? Wanted me like I wanted him?

Because if I was honest with myself, I wanted him so badly I ached, wanted him to take me again like he did last night… but if I let that happen, what would happen to our business deal? And even if it all worked out, could I really be with someone like him? Someone with his need to control?

The way I'd loved submitting to him still disturbed me.

"We need to talk about what happened, don't you think?"

I nodded, a lump rising in my throat.

"One of the things I respect so much about you is your practicality, Rose. You do what needs to be done. You made the difficult decision to accept my offer because of the good you could do with that money. You weighed the discomfort you would feel against the benefit, and your logic prevailed."

I frowned up at him. Where the hell was this going? His patronizing me wasn't a promising sign.

"As much as I loved being with you last night… I think we need to step this back. Keep things professional between us."

His words hit me hard. Even though I had my own doubts about where to go from here, I realized I'd wanted him to say he wanted this. Wanted me. I thought I was ready to hear it, but apparently I wasn't.

Stupid girl. Stupid mistake.

I set my jaw and met his gaze, tamping down my disappointment.

"Okay."

"It's not that I didn't have an amazing time with you, because I did. It's just that I'm trying to simplify my life with this arrangement, not add something that could distract from the campaign. I need to stay focused, now more than ever."

"I understand," I said.

And I did. I was a distraction. A distraction he couldn't afford. As shitty as it made me feel, I understood. He couldn't risk his heart as much as I couldn't risk mine. We were alike, after all. We just had different reasons for keeping a distance.

He assessed me for a long while, his eyes never leaving mine, as if he was trying to read my thoughts. He touched his lip with one finger, then finally sighed and dropped his hand.

"You're an amazing woman, Rose. Thank you for your understanding. I mean that."

I nodded, and turned back to my work, laying out serving spoons and tongs for my short ribs.

"How can I help?"

He was still right beside me, tying on an apron. He wasn't just here to blow me off, then. The weight in my chest lightened a bit. I respected that.

"Carry these serving trays out to the dining room? I'll be right behind you."

He moved with grace, picking up both trays piled with food like they weighed nothing. He gave me a smile as he left the room, and I felt my heartbeat speed up despite myself.

Why couldn't things ever be simple?

At the end of the night, I grinned, watching Jordan devour his polenta, after kicking up his usual fuss about how "weird" it looked. Lana was back, sitting at the edge of the hall, eating quietly at the end of one table. She looked up and I waved to her. She smiled shyly, the look on her face warming me from head to toe.

Jackson was right beside me, his apron spotted with grease, his perfect hair mashed under a hairnet, looking sexier than ever. He leaned over and whispered in my ear, over the chatter of the dining room.

"How would you feel about getting married on May 1st?"

"May what? That's three weeks from now."

"Is that a problem?"

I stared at him, my mouth suddenly very, very dry.

"I… I just… No, it's not a problem. Sounds good."

"Of course, there will be a wedding planner, and my campaign manager will make sure everything is taken care of. You don't have to do anything you don't want to do, but I also want you to feel comfortable putting your touches on things if you'd like. You're the bride, after all."

"I'm the bride…"

I swallowed hard, trying not to show the panic welling up inside of me.

"I'm sure you've been thinking about your perfect wedding since you were a girl."

"Honestly… I've never even thought about it."

He raised an eyebrow. "Oh? I thought all little girls planned their dream weddings."

What could I say to that? That I had bigger things to think about, like where my next meal was coming from? That my daydreams consisted of having parents who loved me instead of flowers and gowns?

"I guess I'm not like most girls."

"That is definitely true," he said, smiling. "That's why I chose you, after all."

I felt the heat rising in my cheeks. The way he looked at me was making me want him all over again, despite my best intentions.

"I'll put you in touch with the wedding planner, then. You'll need a dress, of course, but all the little details will be taken care of for us by the best of the best. All I need you to do is notify whoever you want attending on your side. Of course I'll cover any travel expenses, so invite whoever you'd like."

"I…"

I stared out over the crowd of kids. Who would I invite? I didn't know anyone except for the people here and some acquaintances from my job. Other than that, I had no one. Well, there was my foster mother, but I didn't know if I could face her. Not when the whole thing was a lie.

"May I invite some of the kids?"

"Of course."

Jackson was close now, his hand on the small of my back again, as if he couldn't help but touch me. I pressed my lips together, trying to tamp down the jolt of pleasure I felt at his caress.

"They don't have anything to wear…"

"I'll make sure they're taken care of."

I looked up into his eyes, suddenly realizing what I'd have to do.

"I'll have to lie to them. I mean… about this marriage. About us."

"Don't think of it as a lie, Rose," he said. "Think of it as a way to help them."

His tone was soothing, but his words made me furrow my brow. He spoke so confidently, so casually about the lie, that suddenly, I wondered what I really knew about this man. How much of him was the politician, willing to do anything to win, and how much was the idealistic D.A. determined to help the community?

I shrugged away from his hand and carried away the empty trays.

I had a lot of thinking to do, and not a lot of time to do it. After all, there was a wedding to plan.

Jackson asked me to dinner the next night, and when the car pulled up to my doorstep, my heart jumped to my throat. I wore another of the dresses Madeline sent me home with, a swingy blue cocktail dress that she said brought out my eyes, but I felt anything but confident. I suspected tonight was the night Jackson would propose, and the thought of reacting convincingly, in public no less, made my stomach clench.

I slipped into the backseat. Jackson was already there, looking fantastic as usual in a dark suit and tuxedo shirt, unbuttoned at the collar. I gave him a tight-lipped smile as we pulled away from the curb.

Jackson took my hand in his, and my whole body reacted, the feel of him electric. I cursed myself inwardly, wishing I could do something to break the spell he put on me. I didn't want to meet his eyes, didn't want these emotions coursing through me, arousal and sadness mixing into something almost overwhelming.

I couldn't be with him like that, so why was he teasing me?

He squeezed my hand, and I looked up. He nodded toward the driver, then kissed the back of my hand. I remembered where else those lips had been, and shivered.

The driver. Of course we have to act like we're in love. One slip up, and the whole charade would be exposed.

We rode in silence, hand in hand, as I tried to ignore the sexy way his hair stood up on his head and the alluring scent of his cologne. I sought to distract myself, thinking about how five million dollars could change my life.

I knew I wanted to fund the center for sure. Maybe I could invest one or two million to keep funds flowing toward the programs. I could set it up so it was self-perpetuating, and finally be free to focus on helping wherever I pleased. I could spend all day cooking or spending time with the younger teens, helping them the way I wished someone had helped me. The thought was a comforting one.

My last foster mother was a godsend, and I could only imagine what my life would have been like if I'd only met her earlier. She took a fragile, anxious 15-year-old girl and turned her into a woman with her patience and unrequited love. Regina Jones was a godly woman, and even though I never found religion, she showed me what it meant to care for others and how giving to others could help heal a wounded soul.

I still remember her hanging up the dress she made for me me in my closet and finding my cache of hidden food, stolen from her pantry. I thought she would be furious, would beat me like others had, but she looked at me, standing behind her, rail thin with knotted fists, ready to fight back, and the kindness in her eyes took my breath away.

She put a hand on each of my shoulders and looked straight into my eyes.

"Honey, you don't have to be afraid of going hungry here," she said. "I'm blessed to have you as my daughter now, and I take care of my own. Always."

I looked at her with suspicious eyes until she brought me into an embrace so tight, so real, I did something I never thought I'd do. I hugged her back, tears stinging my eyes.

That night she gave me my first cooking lesson, showing me how to cook collard greens using the leftover pork neck from the other night's meal and letting me brown the beef for the meatloaf. For the first time in years, I remember laughing as she told me stories from her childhood, each time relating them back to the food we prepared together.

After that, I was by her side every Friday night, preparing meals to take to the poor folk in the community, several who couldn't afford to eat on the weekends, when the local food bank was closed.

If I could help anyone like Regina helped me, my life would have purpose. Especially if I could do it in a way that lasted beyond my time on earth. Money could make that dream a reality.

Jackson was watching me carefully when I looked over at him, and I glanced away. I had to get my head together if I was going to play the part of a thrilled fiancée tonight. He hit a button on the console, and a screen went up between us and the driver with a mechanical whir.

"How are you holding up?"

"I'm nervous," I said.

Why lie?

"I'm sure you already suspect this, but tonight I'd like to propose somewhere where we'll be seen, so the media can report on it as soon as possible. Besides, we need to get a ring on your finger."

I chewed my lip. It was surreal that he could talk about this and be so cold. So business-like. But that's what he did every day. Even though I believed his convictions, that didn't mean he didn't deceive people or spin things to get what he wanted.

"I thought so."

"But, before dinner, I thought we could have a little fun together," he said.

"Fun?"

"Absolutely."

He smiled at me in a way that made my heart ache and my pulse throb between my legs.

"Even if we're being professional about this arrangement, there's no reason we can't enjoy ourselves."

The car slowed, and I gazed out the tinted windows, wondering what he possibly had in store for me. A bright storefront made me gasp as my eyes wandered over the elegant window display. It was William Sonoma, the place that made me drool just thinking about it. The place that was too expensive for me to even set foot in without freaking out about breaking something.

We got out of the car, and Jackson tucked my arm beneath his, smiling warmly.

"I thought instead of going to some stuffy restaurant, we could do a little wine tasting here, then stay for the cooking class. What do you say, Rose? Are you up to introducing me into your world tonight?"

I was speechless, a dopey smile frozen on my face as he led me into the store. This was the perfect date, as far as I was concerned, and the fact that he knew that made me tingle all over.

"Can I tell you a secret?" he said. "I've never cooked a day in my life. Well, not unless you count making toast."

I laughed, giving him a playful shove.

"You've got to be joking."

"It's sad, but true. So I'm counting on you to make sure I don't set myself on fire, or worst case scenario, poison us both."

"No problem, Jacks," I said. "I've got your back."

He smiled down at me. His smile was casual, but his eyes betrayed him. He wanted me. Wanted me badly, and even now, in the middle of the store, I thought he might grab me and kiss me hard, stealing my breath away.

"Welcome to William Sonoma," a young man in an apron said. "Oh, my God! You're that guy running for Governor, aren't you? Pierce, right?"

Jackson smiled brightly. "Guilty as charged."

"Oh, wow. We've never had anyone famous in here before…
uh… Are you here for the wine tasting, or looking for anything
special, Mr. Pierce, Sir?"

"Both," Jackson said, giving me a heated look.

"Okay, um, this is so exciting... Please come this way, and we'll
get you started."

I suppressed a laugh at the blush creeping up the man's neck as
he tried to remain professional, and we followed him to the back of
the store. Behind the counter, a woman stared, mouth-open as she
took our picture with her iPhone.

So this was what it was like in Jackson Pierce's world. I had to
admit… it was kind of fun.

We drank wine as we walked around the multi-level store,
talking and laughing, me explaining to him what all of the kitchen
gadgets were for, and him looking like he was soaking up every
minute, his eyes watching my mouth as I smiled, the hunger I saw
before muted now, but still present. He was going to make life
difficult for me, I just knew it, but in this setting, I couldn't muster
up the worry. It was just too awesome.

People stared, and employees whispered behind their hands,
taking surreptitious videos with their phones. Jackson ignored them
like a pro, unless someone approached him directly. If they did, the
charm was on in a flash, and he was shaking hands and patting
shoulders like they were old friends. It was bizarre to watch.

While he talked with an elderly couple, I eyed the KitchenAid
mixers and sighed. I would give anything to replace my ancient
hand mixer and use something more industrial when I made meals
for the kids, but at a starting price of almost $400, looking was all I
was going to do.

I traced my hand over a sky blue mixer before moving on with
Jackson to try a different wine, this one a bubbly white from Peru.
The woman serving almost dropped the bottle on the ground when
she saw Jackson approaching, giggling and smiling at him like a
school girl meeting her favorite pop star.

"I love your ads," she said, her voice high and breathless. "You're even taller in person."

She sighed dreamily and handed him a glass, then stared at me as if just realizing I was there. After a glower, she poured me a glass as well. I rolled my eyes when she turned her back. I mean, I knew Jackson was handsome and powerful, definitely a winning combination, but this was getting ridiculous.

When the cooking class started, I was pleasantly buzzed and having a wonderful time, although there was still a teeny tiny pit in my stomach when I thought about what was coming. I tried to distract myself, hanging strips of fresh pasta on the rack with Jackson, and actually forgot all about it once his fettuccini noodles stuck together in a hopeless tangle. I laughed, and came to his rescue, helping him roll out a new batch of pasta.

After a surprisingly good dinner, we went out for drinks at the bar down the street, a posh place with a large outdoor balcony overlooking the city, twinkle lights in the trees making it seem like we were floating among the stars.

Once again, we were surrounded by people asking to shake hands and take pictures. Jackson smiled, making flawless small talk as I stared, anxious and unsure of what to do with my hands. I settled for fiddling with my clutch bag and trying not to get pushed out of the way. Finally, the patrons filtered off, back to their drinks and conversations, and we were finally alone.

Jackson ordered two martinis, and we sat together, overlooking the boulevard below, people watching as we sipped our drinks. Despite the crowds, the evening had been one of the best dates of my life. None of the men I'd dated before ever asked about my interests, much less framed an evening around them.

"It's hard to believe this is all fake."

His hand on my knee startled me, and I realized I'd spoken my thoughts aloud. He didn't speak, but stroked my knee with his thumb, sending shivers straight down to my toes. Behind us, music started playing.

"Dance with me."

It wasn't a request, not that I would have refused. At that moment, I just wanted to touch him, as stupid as that sounds. I wanted to be close to him. To feel his heat mingling with my own. The pull between us was magnetic. Primal. I needed to be in his arms just then, even if it made me feel things I should repress.

He pulled me out of my chair and led me out to the middle of the patio where other couples swayed together. His hand on the small of my back felt just right, like I'd been built just for him, and as he pulled me close, I sighed at the feel of his body pressed against mine, my hand captured in his.

He moved even closer, pressing his cheek to mine. A light layer of stubble whispered against me, the feel of his breath on my neck making me tremble through and through. A pulse beat between my legs, and suddenly, all I could think about was the way he took me before, rough and hard; the way I felt when he was inside of me, his hands holding my wrists captive.

His lips touched my neck, soft and warm. I sighed and leaned against him, arousal coursing through me. What was he doing? Here? Now? I tightened my grip on his shoulder, my nails digging into his jacket as he kissed me again, the sensation slow and agonizingly sexy.

His cheek slid over mine as he pulled back. When he kissed me, my lips parted for him, and his tongue slid over mine, making my whole body catch fire. I moaned into his mouth as he pulled me even closer, crushing me to him as we danced.

He kissed me harder, still slow, but now I could tell he was exercising all his restraint, trying not to take it too far. When we broke away, I was breathless, my chest heaving against his.

He gestured to someone behind me, and I looked up, confused. A server came up to us holding a dozen crimson roses. Jackson took them with a 'thank you,' and before I knew what was happening, he was on one knee, smiling up at me in a way that made my knees weak.

"Rose, I wanted you to have this bouquet tonight, so you understand in some small way how beautiful you are to me."

He offered the roses, and I took them numbly, staring down at him, frozen like a deer in the headlights. Waiters and patrons alike stared, but the musician kept playing, and suddenly, I realized the melody had changed. Now, instead of the song we'd been dancing to, the first notes of "Kiss from a Rose" filled the evening air.

Jackson took my hand in his, and even though I knew better, tears stung the corners of my eyes.

"These roses, as gorgeous as they are, can't possibly match even one look from you, one moment in your presence. You are beautiful inside and out, Rose Turner, and when I'm with you, I know I can be better than I am. Because you are everything I've ever wanted in a woman, in a partner… in a best friend."

A tear rolled down my cheek as he squeezed my hand, the perfume of the roses filling my senses, my mind overwhelmed by his words, even though I knew, deep down, that none of this was real. That it was all just for show. I'd be a fool to think otherwise, even for a second.

"Rose, I know this is all happening quickly, and I know it seems crazy, but I can't stand another minute without asking you to be mine for as long as I live. I need you, Rose. And I hope you need me."

He drew a carved wooden box out of his pocket and held it up as an offering.

"If you take this ring… if you agree to spend your life with me… I promise to spend every day, each waking moment from now on, trying to make you the happiest woman on earth. I love you more than words can say."

His voice hitched, and I bit my lip.

"Rose… Will you marry me?"

It was all too much, too real, too close to home. The music swelled, the chorus haunting and beautiful, the words enfolding me, even as Jackson's proposal sunk in. I realized I was crying full out now, and I dropped to my knees, hugging him so hard I almost knocked him over.

"Yes."

I kissed him with everything I had, pouring out all of my confusion, my lust, and my heartache into that one, passionate, heady moment. He held me tight, kissing me back, salt mingling on our lips as my tears rolled down.

The bar erupted in raucous cheers, applause and whoops of joy surrounding us.

Jackson looked at me, holding my face with one hand, his expression of happiness so genuine, that for a moment I allowed myself to be swept away.

He loves me. I love him.

Then, he pulled me to my feet, and opened the jewelry box. A cushion-cut diamond the size of a dime nearly blinded me. I made a wheezing noise, and Jackson laughed, before slipping it onto my finger and kissing me on the nose.

"It suits you," he said.

And just like that, people were clapping us on the shoulder, strangers were hugging me, and camera phones snapped pictures all around us. The server brought us chilled champagne, and Jackson tipped him with what looked like a hundred dollar bill. It was totally overwhelming, and I chugged my first glass of bubbly, trying not to lose it.

At least you were convincing, I thought. At least you didn't blow it.

The music changed to another song, and soon we were dancing again, holding one another close, me burying my face in his shoulder, trying not to think about the fact that it was all lies, all bullshit, all just a business deal.

These feelings weren't real. They weren't real. They weren't real.

There was no way I could be falling for Jackson Pierce. It would ruin everything if I were, so I wasn't. I couldn't be, and that was all there was to it.

"You're incredible," Jackson whispered.

He pulled back, smiling down at me. When I saw the look in his eyes, I knew. I was in way over my head. This marriage was trouble, and there was nothing I could do about it.

I held Jackson close, and tried not to think about the days to come.

CHAPTER 15

The partition was up on the drive back, but Jackson held my hand anyway. I tried not to stare down at the almost comically large diamond ring glinting on my finger, but my eyes were drawn to it. It was the nicest thing I'd ever owned by far. Hell, it probably cost more than a college tuition, but at least for now, I couldn't feel guilty. He'd given it to me, and tonight, it was beautiful, and nothing else.

"I mean it, you know," Jackson said.

"Mean what?"

"It really does look good on you."

He grinned at my expression. He'd caught me checking it out, and he knew it.

"I had a great time tonight," I said. "I don't know what I expected, but… not that. I mean, I know it had to look real, so… good job."

What could I say? That no one had ever made me feel the way I did tonight? That no man had ever been so thoughtful? That even when Jackson Pierce was faking, he was better than any real date I'd ever experienced?

He squeezed my hand.

"It's effortless with you," he said. He looked past me, his eyes distant. "With the women I've seen, it was always… different. Harder."

"Even with the women at the club?"

He stiffened beside me, and immediately I regretted my words. After all, this was what he was desperately trying to cover up. His past. His scandalous affairs and unusual appetites.

"I'm sorry, Jackson. Forget I asked."

He looked at me for a long while, his eyes thoughtful.

"I think that's why I went to the club in the first place. With the women there, it was uncomplicated. No emotion, no attachments, no dates or detail work. It was simple."

I looked down at our hands, still entwined, not knowing how to respond.

"Seems you do well with fake girlfriends," I finally said.

I laughed nervously.

"That's different. You're different."

"It's just the other side of the same coin, isn't it? Passion without a relationship, or a relationship without passion..."

What was wrong with me? Why couldn't I just shut up already?

Jackson looked at me again, his brow furrowed.

"I wanted to make you happy tonight."

"I..."

"Don't you see, Rose?"

His voice was low and dangerous. He leaned forward and ran his thumb over my cheek, his touch electric.

"I didn't have to. I know what this is, but I needed to make you happy tonight."

He was so close now, I worried he could hear the frantic beating of my heart.

"What are you doing to me?"

His hand moved down to my neck, his fingers trailing down my skin. I whimpered, looking into those dark eyes of his, his words echoing my own thoughts. What were we doing? What was this attraction that was so hard to resist, despite our best intentions?

His fingers wrapped in my hair, and he tilted my head back roughly. I gasped.

"What are you fucking doing to me?"

His voice was rough, raw, his eyes glinting like a predator's. Before I could say anything, his lips were on my neck, his tongue tasting me, making my whole body quake. He held me captive, but I didn't want to escape. When his hand snuck up my thigh beneath the hem of my dress, I groaned, my body already wet for him.

My restraint was gone, left back on the dance floor of the bar, and I reached for him, running my hands up his chest, loving the feel of his hard muscles beneath my fingers.

He growled in my ear.

"I want you, Rose."

I whimpered as his hand crept higher. His fingers brushed my panties, making me squirm against the leather upholstery. His mouth met mine, his teeth rasping over my lips. He bit down, and I moaned.

He rubbed me, teasing me through the thin cotton covering my sex, rubbing my folds in a way that made me pant as he held me fast, his hand still fisted in my hair. I needed to touch him back, to please him. I reached down and felt him, hard as steel beneath his slacks. His erection twitched against me, and he exhaled.

The car rolled to a stop. Jackson sat back, breathing hard, and adjusted himself just as we heard the driver's door slam shut. I patted my hair down and jerked down on the hem of my skirt. My door opened, and the driver smiled at us. His eyes landed on the ring, and his face lit up.

"Are congratulations in order, Mr. Pierce?"

"Yes, Matthew. You're looking at my gorgeous fiancée."

"Well done, both of you," he said, helping me out of the car, then wringing my hand. "What wonderful news."

Mr. Pierce shut the door behind him, and took my arm.

"Thank you very much, but if you'll excuse us…"

"Of course, Sir! Have a good rest of your night."

The driver gave us a wink and a grin before Jackson rushed me into the house, breezing past the butler with a curt "Good evening," and ushering me up the stairs like we were escaping a fire.

At the landing, he scooped me up, and I shrieked as he threw me over his shoulder. Once in the master suite, he slammed the door and pressed my back against it, pinning me with his arms. The look on his face, bald, animal lust, was almost frightening, especially compared to his usual, public calm.

"Tell me you want this."

I panted, my whole body a live wire, thrumming in anticipation over giving myself to him. Of giving up control, just one more time, and letting myself submit. To him, to my own desire… Just for one more night before sanity set in once more.

"Yes," I breathed.

That was all it took.

He pressed against me, holding me to the door, his body a restraint, his erection grinding against me as his lips met mine. I wanted to wrap my hands around him, but they were at my sides, helpless as he took my mouth, his kisses rough. Aggressive.

When he pulled away, his eyes trailed down my body.

"Take it off now, or I rip it off," he growled.

I fumbled for my zipper, and pulled it down. The look in his eyes told me he meant business, but this was too nice a dress to destroy. I slid it down, shaking under his gaze, my need for him so powerful I thought I might explode if he didn't touch me soon. The heat between my legs pulsed for him.

He grabbed the dress out of my hands and tossed it to the floor by the platform bed. I unclasped my bra with trembling hands, and he scowled with impatience. He sprang forward and grabbed my panties, pulling them down so fast, I gasped, then picking me up. I yelled as he tossed me onto the bed.

"Open your legs."

His tone brooked no argument. I stared up at him, anxiety coursing through me. I wanted him so badly, I thought I might die if he didn't take me now, but the thought of opening myself to him, of letting him see me like this, naked and vulnerable, spread out before him, was terrifying.

"Rose," he said. "Trust me."

I looked up a the man standing above me, the man who just gave me one of the best night's of my life, and realized that deep down, I did trust him. I trusted him more than I'd trusted anyone in a long, long time.

I opened my legs for him, leaning back on my elbows, letting him see me, my nipples peaking, my bare folds exposed to his scrutiny. He looked me up and down, his eyes glinting, a wolfish grin on his face. He was so different like this… so raw. So wicked.

This was the real Jackson Pierce—what lived beneath his polished exterior. A beast of a man with a ravenous hunger. His eyes told me he wanted to devour me. To swallow me whole and make me part of his dark little world.

I moaned as he knelt at the edge of the bed and pushed my thighs apart. He ripped open his shirt, buttons flying off to the dark corners of the room, and shrugged it onto the floor.

"Put your hands above your head and clasp them together," he commanded. "Don't move them. You're mine tonight, and you'll do exactly what I say. Understand?"

"Yes," I whispered.

"Yes, what."

"Yes… Sir."

The word felt like a kiss.

He grinned again, devilish in the warm light of his bedside lamp, his face half in shadow, white teeth glinting.

"Do not cum until I tell you, Rose. Your pleasure belongs to me."

Before I could ask what he meant, he lowered his mouth between my legs. I gasped and fell back on the duvet, clasping my hands hard together over my head, just like I was told.

His tongue traced me, parting me, tasting my arousal. He groaned into me, the vibration sending white-hot sparks through my core. I clenched my hands, wanting to touch him, feeling so vulnerable, even though I knew all I had to do was disobey, and I would be free to cover myself, to push him away.

But I needed to do what he demanded. Needed to please him. Needed to give myself over to his will, at least for tonight.

I leaned back and closed my eyes, whimpering as he laved me again and again.

"You taste so fucking good," he groaned. "I knew you would."

I bit my lip, my cheeks burning up at his words. No one had ever said anything like that to me before. The soles of my feet flexed as he found my clit, sucking and licking in a way that made me want to scream. I struggled to keep my hands where they were, trapping myself, even as he trapped me with his words.

"Don't," he said.

He lowered his mouth, chuckling against me even as he wrapped his lips over my clit again.

I struggled against the wave of pleasure building strength inside of me, swelling bigger and bigger, threatening to crash down and drown me if I wasn't careful. I mewled, writhing on the sheets, but he held me fast, his hands bruising my thighs.

He nudged me with his nose, and I moaned louder, biting my lip so hard it hurt, trying to hold back, to keep myself under control. For him.

"Cum," he said. "Cum for me, beautiful girl. Cum for me now."

He suckled me hard, flicking me again and again with his tongue.

I cried out his name as I gave myself over, releasing my pleasure for him, at his command. I shook against his hands as I convulsed, my pussy squeezing again and again as my orgasm swept me away. I hit the pillows above me with my clasped hands, wanting to hold him to me, but stilled by his words. By his will.

"Good girl," he said against me, his breath cool on my hot, needy flesh.

He pulled away, releasing me, and my legs fell, limp, onto the bed. I felt wrung out, but at the same time, needier than ever. I craved him. Wanted him inside of me, filling me to the brim.

"Please," I said. "Please."

Jackson stripped off his pants and let them fall to the ground. His boxer briefs outlined him perfectly, proud and hard, waiting to be set free. I licked my lips watching him, and he grinned.

"Do you want this?"

He traced the line of his erection, gripping his shaft through the cotton. My body convulsed again just looking at it. He was so bold, so totally unashamed. So fucking sexy, it almost hurt to look at him.

"Yes! God, yes…"

I would beg him for it if I had to.

He rubbed himself, watching me carefully, studying me as I sat up on the bed, then walked over. He inched his underwear down until the head of his gorgeous cock jutted out above the elastic. A bead of pre-cum glistened at the tip. He saw me staring, open-mouthed and panting, and scooped up the bead up with his middle finger.

He pressed the finger to my lips until I opened for him, suckling him into my hot mouth. I licked him clean, groaning at the salty taste of him. Of Jackson. He held out another finger, and I sucked them greedily, the contact making me hotter than ever, my arousal leaking out onto my thighs.

He slid his fingers slowly out of my mouth, looking at me like he wanted nothing more than to fill my mouth with something else entirely, his eyes dark with desire. I opened my lips, ready to take him in, ready to please him the same way he pleased me, wanting so badly to feel him inside of me, even this way.

He pulled away, lowering his underwear, but stayed where he was, looking me over, his eyes moving over my naked body. I wanted to reach for him, to stroke him, but something told me to stay where I was. He was in charge. Every cell in my body knew that, and the knowledge made me feel wild. Free. Sexual in a way I'd never felt before.

"I want to bind you," he said, his voice low and harsh. "Will you trust me that way?"

His words made my eyes widen, but at that point, I wanted anything he had to give me. I was his tonight. Wholly his, and nothing could make me stop trusting him.

"Yes, Sir," I breathed.

He grinned again, pleased that I'd remembered.

"Come to me."

I stood on wobbly legs and walked over to him, wondering what on earth he had in store for me.

He removed a silk scarf from his dresser drawer, the same one where I'd nicked his boxers and t-shirt, and led me to one of the bedposts at the bottom of the bed. He pushed me roughly against the wooden post and stood behind me, his body so close I could feel his heat.

"Put your arms above your head."

I did as I was told, stretching my wrists above my head, my body alert and alive, waiting for him to touch me. To use me. To give me pleasure even as he took his own. To make my world turn upside down again, like it had the first night we were together.

Jackson teased me, running the scarf slowly up my arms, the silk whispering against my skin. Goosebumps arose, and I shivered at the touch. He bound first one wrist, then the other, then looped the middle over the small, metal hooks that held the canopy. My feet still touched the floor, but I realized I couldn't unhook myself, even if I stood on tip-toe. All I could do was grab the scarf above my wrists and hang on. I was completely at his mercy.

He moved forward, pressing his erection against my ass, the feeling like velvet over an iron rod, smooth and hard all at once. His breath was on my neck, and for a moment, he just stood there, towering above me, hemming me in, hulking and dangerous, and oh-so-delicious. Adrenaline coursed through me, waiting for him to do something, say something.

Finally, I felt his teeth on my neck. He nipped me just enough for it to hurt, and I moaned, pressing back into him.

"God, you're beautiful," he said.

He kissed my neck where he'd bitten me, soothing the sting. His hands ran over my back, caressing the curve of my waist, loving my shape, and dipping down to the curve just above my ass, before kneading my round cheeks, spreading me open from behind. He touched my folds, slick and ready, and groaned.

I felt him adjust himself behind me, and moaned softly, the thrill of anticipation coursing through me like fire. He pressed a palm onto my lower back, making me arch downward and back toward him, holding onto the silk that bound me to support my weight. I mewled, suddenly afraid, tied like this, hanging, but when

I felt the thick tip of his cock pressing into me, fear turned to a longing so intense, tears stung my eyes.

He eased into me, still pressing me down, and groaned, his voice a harsh rasp behind me.

"Fuck. You're so tight, Rose…"

Strong hands gripped the top of my ass, pulling me back onto him with a grunt. The silk pulled tight, and I lifted up on the balls of my feet, unable to hold myself up, leaning back, supported between my bonds and the man behind me. I cried out as he impaled me again, hard and rough, pulling me onto him even as he slammed his shaft home, filling me almost to the point of pain.

"Do you love this?" He demanded. "Do you love my fucking cock in you?"

"Yes," I moaned.

"Tell me how much you love being drilled by my thick fucking cock…"

"I…"

It was hard to obey, hard to do anything other than feel as he picked up the pace, riding me from behind, bucking into me so hard that I was lifted up a little with each stroke, bouncing on the balls of my feet.

"Tell me!"

He swatted my ass, and I gasped, the sting of his hand mingling with the feel of him inside of me, the sweet friction unbearably right, unbearably bringing me higher and higher toward that peak once again.

"I love your cock," I cried. "I love your thick fucking cock, Sir!"

"God, yes," he growled.

He thrust harder, again and again, my breasts swaying as he held me tight, making me his. When he wrapped an arm around my waist and held me tight to his belly, my mind was wild, an animal mind, all coherent thought replaced by heat and sex and wanting.

He held one of my thighs with his other arm, supporting me as I leaned against my restraints, then used the first hand to stroke my clit, rubbing me again and again as he pounded into me.

"Not until I tell you."

I moaned in agreement, my head thrown back, giving myself over to the sensations flowing through me, over me, around me. I was surrounded by him, inside and out, my body his for the taking, and me the grateful giver.

He pistoned hard and fast, his thickness making me ache to cum, his fingers on my clit making it almost impossible to hold back. I wailed, frustrated, and he bit my neck again, fucking and stroking and holding me until I didn't think I could take any more.

"Now!"

I broke apart, screaming as he stroked into me again and again and again, my body shattering as he held me tight, milking him, needing him to cum inside of me on a level so primal it bordered on instinct.

He clenched me to him hard, crushing me into him as he cried out. I felt him inside of me, filling me with his warmth, twitching as his orgasm took him to the place where I was still flying, bringing us together to soar, body to body, on pleasure's wings.

Later, as we lay together in his bed, tangled in one another's arms, I kissed him softly on the chest. He held me tighter and pressed his lips to my hair.

"I thought you said this marriage would be strictly business," I said, smiling.

"Politicians lie, Rose."

I laughed, and lay back against, him, enjoying the moment. Before long, though, as his breathing deepened, my smile faded, and I stared at the starlight filtering in through the window.

What did he mean by that? Was he just making a joke, or was it something else?

I shifted off him, and he rolled to the side, murmuring, but not waking up. I walked into the master bathroom and shut the door quietly. I filled a glass of water, and drank it down, hoping to calm my racing thoughts. Maybe I was just tired. Just imagining things.

Maybe I was just shaken up because I hadn't trusted someone like this in a long, long time, and certainly never a lover. The only person I'd trusted not to hurt me was Regina, and that took time to build. So why was I falling into Jackson's arms so fast, when I knew it could all blow up?

Especially when this was supposed to be business. Shady business at that.

He was a liar, and so was I. This whole arrangement was a lie, a farce to fool the press into thinking he wasn't some bad boy sex maniac. And yet here I was, letting him tie me to the bedpost, when I really didn't even know him.

I looked in the mirror, my face strange, alien, in the blue glow from the nightlight by the sink.

I put my glass down and ran the water, splashing my face and trying to focus on just breathing. I had to remember that no matter what I felt, no matter how irresistible this man seemed, no matter what kind of connection we had since the moment we met, it was all fake. All just a show that went one step too far. We'd gotten carried away, and now I thought that I could trust him.

That I could even love him.

I stood back up and slicked my hair back, looking at my own reflection. Haunted eyes stared back at me from a drawn face.

What had I gotten myself into?

CHAPTER 16

A couple of days later, I picked Lana up outside of her apartment complex, still feeling out of sorts, my thoughts reeling whenever I thought of my night with Jackson. The proposal had thrown me for a loop all right, but now I at least had a grip on my emotions again.

I mean, who wouldn't get confused in a situation like this? It was natural that feelings would crop up, but that didn't have to mean anything. At least not anything real. Not anything you could put your faith in.

I just had to remember that.

Lana bounded down the apartment stairs as soon as I pulled up. She looked smaller than ever, but when she saw me, her eyes widened, her whole face lighting up.

"You came," she said.

Her voice was quiet, and her tiny hands fidgeted in front of her soiled dress.

"Of course I did."

I smiled warmly and held my hand out for her. She grasped it eagerly.

"When I say we're having a girls day out, I mean it." I winked at her. "We're doing the works today—dress shopping, shoe shopping and a nice lunch. Are you ready to have some fun?"

She giggled and nodded her head, her lank blonde hair hanging around her face.

"Thank you for agreeing to be my flower girl, Lana. It will be great to have you by my side on the big day."

We walked to the car, hand in hand.

"Do you think you'll get scared?" she said.

I looked down at her in surprise. Was I that obvious?

"Maybe. I hear brides sometimes get nervous before they walk down the aisle…"

This kid had no idea. I was freaking out just thinking about it.

"But you love him? Mr. Jackson?"

I smiled down at her. Somehow, her hand in mine calmed me, even as I prepared to answer her questions with lies. I was doing this for her and the others at the center. I supposed I could endure a little discomfort to make our dreams come true.

"Very, very much," I said.

The little girl smiled shyly. "Why?"

"Why? What kind of question is that?"

I grinned and gave her hand a squeeze. Her face fell, her eyes wide and shining.

"I dunno," she said. "I just wondered what it was like."

I opened the car door for her and she slid inside. I frowned as I walked to my side of the car, hoping she didn't see the worry on my face. I suppose she would want to know why people loved one another. From what I knew about her, she was a runaway from an abusive home. There couldn't have been a whole lot of love in her life up until now.

Poor kid. I knew all too well what that felt like.

"Well," I said, starting the car and pulling onto the road. "He's handsome, for starters."

Lana giggled again, staring at me with rapt attention.

"He's kind and strong, and he always tries to do the right thing. He cares very much about the people around him, even if he doesn't know them."

"He does?"

I smiled now, my eyes on the road, but my mind on Jackson Pierce. There really was a lot to love, and being honest about those things would only make my words more believable. My heart ached thinking about him like that, so soon after I promised myself to keep my distance. I couldn't let myself get hurt. Not like that. Not again.

"He does, and that's very rare, Lana. Most people only care about their family or their friends. It takes a special kind of person to care about helping strangers. He's one of those special people, which is why I care so much about him."

I thought about the way he worked side by side with me, without a camera crew in sight. He was there to be seen, sure, but part of me wondered if he just enjoyed the work. The idea made my heart do a little flip in my chest, but I quickly tamped it down.

"Plus, he sees the best in people, even if they don't see it themselves."

You're perfect, Rose...

The memory of his words made my stomach clench. I felt Lana's eyes on me, watching me carefully.

"So that's why I love him." I cleared my throat. "Does that answer your question?"

"I think so," she said. "He makes your heart feel good."

I smiled down at her. "Exactly."

From the mouth of babes.

No matter what I felt, and no matter how smart I tried to be, Jackson did make my heart feel good, even when he was close to breaking it. The fact that I couldn't have him the way I wanted him didn't mean I couldn't appreciate him. But I couldn't give him my heart. I needed to stay skeptical.

We pulled into the bridal shop parking lot, and I glued a smile to my face. No matter what, this wedding was happening, so I'd better get my shit together, and fast.

And even though it was confusing as hell being Jackson's fake bride, this part, being with Lana for the day and showing her a good time, was going to be special. Maybe this wedding wouldn't be such a strain after all.

Hell, with the right attitude, it might even be fun.

I sighed, and turned off the car.

"We'll come out together, okay?"

"I don't want to."

"You'll look beautiful!"

"No... I can't. I look stupid."

"Don't be a baby. We'll go on the count of three..."

I growled from inside my dressing room. This kid was working my last nerve. If I wanted to try on wedding gowns in privacy, that's what I was going to do. The first two looked horrid, but I had a funny feeling when I looked at myself in this third dress. I just didn't know what to do with it.

"One..."

"Knock it off, Lana..."

"Two..."

"You're going to be walking home if you keep this up."

"Three! Let's go!"

I sighed in frustration and pushed open the curtain.

Lana gasped, her small hands flying to her face. She let out a squeal of delight, and I did the same, admiring how different she looked in her cream-colored dress with delicate pink roses around the waist. She looked like a fairy, her hair glowing in the overhead lighting of the boutique.

"You look like a princess," she whispered, her eyes as wide as saucers.

I looked up for the first time and caught a glimpse of myself in the big mirrors. Lana grabbed my hand and dragged me onto the platform in the middle of the mirrors, staring at me the whole way like I was a dream come to life.

Finally, I looked in the mirror full on, and what I saw made me freeze where I stood. Instead of my usual tough-girl façade, the woman reflected back at me was elegant and sensual, the white silk chiffon hugging curves I didn't know I had, the sweetheart top showing me off in a way that took my breath away.

I never in a million years thought I could look like this. Was this real? Or was I dreaming, here with Lana beside me, both of us caught up in this new world, this strange, surreal moment?

Girls like us didn't wear things like this.

Lana tugged on my skirt, waking me from my reverie.

"Put this on."

She handed up a tiara, simple, but more dazzling than anything I'd ever even held in my hands. It was slender and silver, leaves delicately crafted around sparkling flowers made of rhinestones. I slipped it on and let out a shuddering breath as I looked in the mirror. At that moment, I did look like a princess, like the woman I thought I could never be, the beautiful woman who men fought over, and whose only care in the world was what to do that day with her wealth... her freedom. And ruling her kingdom, of course.

I hastily cleared my throat and smiled down at Lana.

"What do you think?"

She grinned, and I noticed a gap where a tooth was missing.

"It's awesome."

I nodded, sneaking one last glance in the mirror.

"What do you think of your dress?"

Lana looked down, touching the cloth roses almost reverently.

"It's expensive," she said.

"Don't worry about that. Do you like it?"

She looked up at me, her eyes big, and chewed her lip.

"Yes."

"Then let's wrap it up and get out of here," I said. "We're going to be two hot babes on May 1st."

"Princesses," Lana said.

"Right, princesses." I smiled and ruffled her hair. "What do you say we get that lunch? Even princesses have to eat."

She giggled and ran back into the changing room.

We left carrying heavy garment bags and arguing about where to go. In the end, I deferred to her decision. Apparently princesses ate pizza.

Good to know.

CHAPTER 17

The day of the wedding dawned clear and warm, but my emotions roiled inside of me like a coming storm. I couldn't believe I'd asked Rose to lie for me, that I'd dared asked anyone to put their life on hold and live this falsehood in front of their friends and family.

Was it worth it? Did the good outweigh the bad? The rumors about my past had been successfully overshadowed by news of the wedding, but it felt wrong. However, I'd come too far to call it off. I couldn't call it off. Not when my entire career rode upon on this moment.

I fastened my cufflinks, feeling sick to my stomach. A strong hand clapped down on my shoulder, and I let out a breath, trying to hide my nerves.

"The first brother to take the plunge. Are you nervous?"

Maxwell, my younger brother, stood beside me, beaming, looking cocky as always.

"No," I lied. "No, not at all."

"Why didn't I ever meet this girl of yours, Jacks? You hide her from us until the wedding day? I mean, were you afraid I'd steal her away with my superior good looks, or what?"

I lowered my eyebrows, giving him a warning gaze.

"When you know, you know. I didn't want to wait. I couldn't let this one get away."

Max put an arm around my shoulder, and gave me a hard squeeze.

"Who are you, and where is my cautious, stick-in-the-mud older brother? This is so unlike you."

I sighed and escaped his grip, smoothing down my tuxedo.

"Do you have the rings?"

"Right here," Max said, patting his pocket.

"And the reading?"

"Lucy's got it covered."

"Okay... okay..."

I paced from one side of the dressing room to the other, looking for my boutonnière.

"Jackson," Max said. "It's going to be fine."

I nodded, absently, still pacing, looking on every surface in the cluttered room. Papers littered the counter in front of the mirror, my vows that I waited until the last minute to memorize because of work. Max's hair cream sat open, the lid four feet away next to his now-empty beer bottle. My mouth felt dry and sand-papery. What I wouldn't give for a drink right now.

As if reading my mind, Max held out a flask.

"You look like you need it."

I smiled and shrugged. "I didn't think I got anxious any more."

"I think your wedding day is just a hair different than giving the same political speech twenty times in a row. Don't worry, though," he said. "It sounds like you're really crazy about this girl. And if you're willing to jump right into marriage, she must be an incredible woman."

I looked up at him, beaming down at me, a dark curl of hair falling over his forehead.

"Besides, I've never known you to make a bad decision, Jacks." He winked at me. "That's my job."

I ran a hand through my hair and gave a half-hearted laugh. I needed to find that damn boutonnière.

"Everyone decent?" My campaign manager, Lisa, burst into the changing room. "Damn, you both are. Anyway, looks like someone would be lost without me."

She held up the single crimson rose and grinned, raising an eyebrow at me.

"You're welcome."

"Lisa, you're a lifesaver," I said, reaching for it.

"Here you go, big boy."

She came close and worked to pin it to my lapel, her tongue sticking out between her teeth as the pin slipped and slid.

"Little bastard... There! Now, you look like a man who's ready to get married."

She smiled up at me.

"Max, could you please have Lucy check on Rose? Make sure everyone's about ready? The ceremony starts in fifteen minutes..."

"No problem," he said. He clapped me on the shoulder. "Make sure he doesn't run, Lisa."

She barked a laugh, and I narrowed my eyes at him. He chuckled and left, closing the door behind him.

"Good news, Jacks," Lisa said, whirling around to face me again. "The gossip columnists are all over that proposal of yours. Some scene you pulled! Everyone loves this kid, and they love you again by default. They've looked into the girl, heard about the charity work, and now they're simply gaga over the whole affair. Not a peep about Miss Whips-n-Chains for days."

I winced internally at her words, but kept my face neutral.

"Well, that is good news."

"This whole thing is working like a charm, just like I said, right? You stick by me, and we'll get you elected yet. Speaking of which, have you thought much about the vows, or are you just going to have the reverend do the boilerplate version?"

I went to the mirror and began tying my thick, silver tie, trying to distract myself. Frankly, Lisa's tone was starting to get under my skin. Even though I knew this was all for the campaign, the last couple of weeks had me thinking maybe Rose and I could be more... were more... that we could work something out after the contract. If I played my cards right, maybe we could see one another during the duration of this marriage...

It was all so complicated. All because of me and my damn campaign.

"We wrote our own," I said.

"Great! I have some notes you can slip in. Just some brief sound bites about your platform. They'll blend right in, but repetition to the voters can't hurt, right?"

She dropped some index cards in front of me covered in her sharp, precise handwriting.

I sighed. "Lisa, I spent all night memorizing these. I'm not adding anything."

"Oh, come on, Jacks. Remember this isn't exactly your real wedding. Keep your eyes on the goal." She leaned back against the counter, scrutinizing me. "I think saying something like 'One thing I loved about you from the start, was that you shared my passion for the Hire More Teachers Act' should do the trick nicely, don't you?"

I stabbed myself with the tie pin, drawing blood. I let out my breath in a hiss.

"Goddamn it, Lisa. Please, I just… I'm all set with the vows I've got. There's plenty of time for sound bites after the wedding. I've got that rally the week after the honeymoon, for Christ's sake."

"Geez, Jacks, calm down," she said, pursing her lips. "If you don't want to take advice from your key advisor, that's your business."

She eyed me up and down, then reached over and straightened my tie. I stiffened beneath her touch, suddenly wishing I hadn't sent Max away.

"Listen, I can see you're stressed. This is a big thing to pull off— I get it. I'll let you be, and if you happen to change your mind, great. If not, no skin off my nose."

She stood and headed for the door, but before she left, she turned back.

"Break a leg out there."

She smiled, but I noticed it didn't reach her eyes. She shut the door with a sharp click, leaving me alone with my thoughts.

I stared at my reflection, wondering what I was missing. I had the tie, the rose, the cufflinks, the vest… Everything was ready. So why did I feel so on edge? I glanced down at the vows again, then at Lisa's notes.

She'd actually written them verbatim for me. They weren't just bullet points of info to work in, but entire, flowery sentences, expressing my love around the brand messaging of my campaign.

My stomach churned, and I sat down for a minute, blowing out a breath. The warmth from my shot from Max's flask was short-lived, and I sat alone, my thoughts spinning, wondering if there was anything in the Bible about using the woman you loved to deceive your voters for the greater good.

It wasn't until Max called me, and we walked up to the alter that I realized what had just gone through my mind.

The woman I loved.

I looked up at the sky, at the majestic evergreens surrounding us in the beautiful outdoor glade we'd set up as a chapel, and prayed that it would all turn out all right.

Please, whoever's out there, I thought. Just don't let her hate me when all of this is over.

That's the one thing I knew I couldn't stand.

CHAPTER 18

"Are you going to barf?"

"Nope," I said, my head between my knees. "I just need a second."

"Because if you're going to barf, I can hold your hair."

Lana stood next to me, peeking under my veil to check on me. I sat up and took a deep, shuddering breath.

"I'm fine. I'm good. I can do this."

I brushed a loose ringlet off her forehead, and she looked up at me with those big eyes of hers full of concern. We were both dressed, my makeup done, and after struggling with a curling iron, she was rocking a head full of adorable curls. I officially had nothing left to do but wait for the ceremony to begin.

There was a tap on the dressing room door, and Lana opened it a crack.

"Is Rose in here, honey?"

Regina's warm voice filtering through the doorway made my heart swell. She was here! I had been on the fence about inviting her, but finally picked up the phone at the last minute, part of me hoping she wouldn't be able to make it, and part of me wanting her here to comfort me more than anything.

Lana looked at me, and I nodded. She opened the door, and my foster mother came in, looking colorful in her Sunday best—a purple skirt suit and matching flowered hat. I loved those hats as a teen and used to try them on in secret, feeling like one of the fancy ladies you saw in movies at the Kentucky Derby.

"Can you give us a few minutes, cutie?"

She smiled down at Lana and gave her cheek a quick brush with her calloused hands, rough from years working as a line cook. I remember watching her fearfully as she lowered chicken cutlets directly into hot oil, the little spatters of grease hitting her skin going unnoticed.

Lana nodded shyly and left the room, closing the door as she went.

"What a sweet girl. Is she one of those kids you love talking about?"

I nodded, my eyes blurring with tears.

"I'm so happy you're here."

"Oh, hush, now. You're going to ruin that pretty makeup."

I choked back a sob and fell into her arms, and she patted my back in a way that brought me back to the nights she held me when I was young and afraid, slowly soothing away my anger until there was nothing left, then filling that empty space with her love.

"Now, why don't you tell me what's going on. I don't want to have to drag it out of you with hardly any time before the big event."

What could I say? I'd formulated lie after lie and discarded them all. She'd see right through me, just like she always did.

"I… I'm getting fake married… for money."

It spilled out before I could stop it, and I gave a squeak of embarrassment. Regina stared at me, her eyebrow up in a way I knew all too well. It was usually followed by a hand on her hip, and when that happened, I knew I was in trouble.

The hand rose and planted itself firmly on a generous curve.

"What's all this now?"

"I don't even know how to say… Where to start…"

I sat down, suddenly feeling small. Fragile.

"Try."

I chewed my lip and tasted the greasy chemical flavor of lipstick. I stopped chewing.

"This politician, Jackson Pierce, offered me a job. If I marry him to help repair his... his reputation, he'll give me five million dollars at the end of one year, and I can go on and live my life however I want... It's all just for show."

"That doesn't sound like any job I've ever heard of."

"I know! I know," I said.

Regina sat next to me and folded her hands in her lap, staring at me, eyebrow still raised skeptically.

"Rumors were flying around about him, and he said because of my community service, I'd make him look good. And at first I didn't want to... it's so stupid, you know? A fake marriage to cover up some B.S. controversy... and I never cared about money before, so why did I care now, right? But then, I started thinking about just how much money that is, I mean really is, and how much good it could do. Permanent good that I just couldn't do any other way."

She let out a sigh and sat back, frowning at me, but the eyebrow lowered.

"Go on."

"I wanted to help the youth center. Set up a foundation. Invest some and live off that, so I could help full time—make more of a difference... I just couldn't turn it down."

"So this is what I came down here for? Your make-believe wedding?"

Her tone was soft now, and I took a deep breath, trying to restore some calm.

Yeah, right. Not today, Rose.

"Yeah, but... that's not all."

Regina leaned forward and lifted my chin up, looking me sternly, right in the eye. My chin trembled in her hand, and she sat back, shaking her head.

"You love him, don't you."

A tear splashed on my cheek. "I don't know," I cried. "This is so stupid!"

"Oh, dear, baby girl," she said. "You are in some kind of trouble."

"D-do you, h-hate me for d-doing this?"

"Oh, Rose."

She stood up and pulled me into her arms, squeezing me tight. She kissed my cheek again and again, until I stopped crying, stilling in her embrace.

"I could never hate you, honey. I understand why you're doing this. You're a good girl. You have a good heart. Always have."

She held me at arm's length.

"Well, we're going to have to fix your face now, but that's okay."

I laughed, a last tear rolling off my lashes.

"But I have one question first. Does this boy feel the same way?"

I sighed, a sob making me hiccup.

"Sometimes I think he… I… I just don't know."

"Well," she said, wetting a paper towel in the sink. "You're a smart girl, so I'll try not to worry. Just promise your old Mom you'll be careful, and I'll believe you."

She handed me the towel, and I blotted at my running mascara.

"I promise. I'll be c-careful."

She patted me on the back, watching me in the mirror.

"I know you will. But remember, too. Don't be so careful that you miss an opportunity that's there. Keep your eyes open, and your heart protected, but ready for what comes, okay?"

"Okay."

I gave her a one-armed hug and kept blotting.

She left me to clean up, promising she'd try to stall the musicians another five minutes or so. I blew my nose and stared at myself, looking like a raccoon in a tiara.

When I heard the first few notes of Pachelbel's Cannon in D, my heart leapt into my throat. The chipper redhead I'd just met, Lucy, was standing in as my maid of honor, looking gorgeous in a lavender gown that made her eyes shine. She smiled encouragingly and squeezed my shoulder.

"Don't worry," she said. "If Jackson is anything like his brother Max, you've got nothing to be nervous about. The Pierce men are pretty amazing."

I fidgeted with my bouquet—a riot of brightly colored roses loosely bunched together, and tried to breathe. Lana started walking, tossing rose petals delicately, and I saw Jackson's brother heading toward us, ready to walk with Lucy. It was almost my turn.

"Yeah, I'm glad I'm putting a ring on it," I said distractedly.

Lucy laughed and elbowed me. "Hell, yeah, put a ring on it!" She shook her head, her curls bouncing, grinning widely. "That's great. I think you and I are going to be good friends. Practically sisters, right?"

"R-right," I said.

I swallowed hard, suddenly wishing I had a water bottle or maybe a fifth of vodka with me.

Max held out his arm to Lucy and gave me a wink. Lucy gave me a quick thumbs up.

"You look beautiful, Rose. Knock 'em dead!"

They walked off, arm in arm, moving slowly between the rows and rows of guests, a bizarre mixture of politicians, business owners and teenagers from the center decked out in new suits and dresses, courtesy of Jackson's credit line.

I saw the back of Kathy's head as she chatted with Regina. Somehow, the sight of those familiar faces calmed me. Helped me take a deep breath and straighten up.

You can do this. It's just a few yards to the altar. You've got this, Rose.

The bridal march began, the bracing chords sending a jolt of adrenaline through me. This was it. Now or never. Do or die…

The crowd rose to their feet, murmuring in excited tones and looking back over their shoulders right at me.

I had a brief fantasy involving kicking off my high heels and making a bee-line for the street, but reigned it in. I put my head up and my shoulders back and focused on walking, one foot in front of the other, to the beat of step, together, pause, step, together, pause.

I could almost feel the gazes landing on me as I walked by, a feeling that gave me the shivers, but when I looked up and saw

Jackson, standing before me in his tuxedo, everyone else faded away.

He looked at me, and the smile on his face transformed into an expression of awe, his eyes shining as they met mine. I suppose I looked at him the same way. As I moved toward him, closing the distance one foot at a time down an endlessly long aisle, I felt his draw, like a magnet connecting to me, like I couldn't get to him quickly enough, to his beautiful self, to be with him, to be touching him again.

I stopped in front of him and stared, not knowing what to do. The pastor said something, and Jackson took my hand in his, the feel of his palm supporting mine surreal in such a scenario, but also so right it brought tears to my eyes.

Lucy tapped me lightly on the shoulder, and nabbed my bouquet when I turned to her, giving me a knowing look. I turned back to Jackson and let him have my other hand. Face to face like this, it was impossibly real, impossibly hard to forget that it wasn't. My heart pounded, and I made sure my knees weren't locked, worried that I'd pass out.

I didn't.

There was a song, then a reading, and then I was following the pastor's lead, stumbling through the vows I'd memorized, muscle memory getting me through as I looked into Jackson's eyes. A pang of guilt stabbed my guts, but I said the words, and he said his. I watched his mouth when he spoke, thinking of him kissing me in his bedroom, of licking and biting, and…

"I now pronounce you man and wife. You may kiss the bride!"

The crowd drew a communal intake of breath, and before I knew what was happening, Jackson grabbed me and dipped me low, kissing me passionately. I threw my arms around his neck and kissed him right back. The crowd burst into cheers and applause, along with some dog-whistles I knew were from my kids.

When I was steady on my own two feet again, I noticed Jackson grinning down at me, some of my lipstick smeared under his bottom lip. I reached up and brushed it off with my thumb, laughing, and he kissed my palm. It felt so natural, being with him, even now.

He led me down the aisle as friends and family cheered, snapping photos and calling out their well-wishes. Before I got to the end, I saw Regina's face. There were tears shining on her cheeks. I didn't know how to feel about that, so I just kept on going. There would be plenty of time to talk later. After all of this craziness was through.

I just hoped she wouldn't worry, even though I knew she would. And that thought more than anything else, made me feel like crying, even as Jackson's hand in mine made me feel like I was the luckiest woman in the world.

CHAPTER 19

Jackson carried me over the threshold to the presidential suite. A room service waiter followed us in with champagne and strawberries, trying to hide a smile and failing miserably. Jackson slipped him what looked like a fifty, and closed the door quickly behind him.

I laughed at the look in his eyes, and sat down on the edge of the bed, feeling like I'd been through the emotional wringer, but pleasantly buzzed, and content in a way I didn't expect. We'd pulled it off, and what was more, I'd actually had fun.

The kids and I busted it out on the dance floor during fast numbers, Joaquin impressing us all with some breakdancing, and Lana bopping to the beat in her fluffy new dress. Jordan even shyly asked for a slow dance, and I obliged, laughing as I accidentally stepped on his feet. Neither one of us knew how to waltz, but we made do. I made sure they all left with something to eat for later after the meal, and when Jackson held me close, nuzzling me like a new husband in love, I sighed, leaning into him, enjoying the moment for as long as it lasted.

I didn't even mind meeting the press members and various government officials who came up to interview and probe and congratulate. I smiled until my face ached, but it was a good ache. The day was beautiful, and the solace of having Regina there, gossiping happily with the mayor's wife in the background, made me feel safe, even though I was definitely out of my depth. I knew I had a lifeline in her, and always would.

Jackson sat on the bed and put an arm around my waist, pulling me to his side. I leaned my head on his shoulder and sighed, a goofy smile on my lips.

"Good work today, Mrs. Pierce," he said.

"Mmm."

He pressed a kiss to my hair, and I let my hand wander onto his knee, wondering what we'd do now that we were alone. Would he make love to me again, like this wedding night was our own? Would he tie me up, or hold me down, and make me cum again and again?

I looked up, and saw him smiling down at me. I tilted my chin until my lips reached his, kissing him softly, our mouths lingering on one another's in a way that made me yearn deep in my soul.

When we broke apart, he held me close, stroking my hair.

"Thank you," he said.

"For what?"

"For this. All of this." He kissed my nose. "For being you."

"My pleasure," I said. "It's something I've gotten pretty good at."

He laughed and held me again, squeezing me so tightly for a moment, I wondered if something was wrong. When he let me go, he looked away and stood up, walking over to the food service cart.

"How about a toast?" he said. "If I'm not mistaken, there's a hot tub on our balcony, Mrs. Pierce. Would you care to break it in with me?"

He grinned, but his eyes were dangerous again, his playfulness masking something far more serious. More primal and hungry and so sexy, it made my breath catch in my throat.

He picked up two champagne flutes and the bucket and headed to the balcony, eying me in a way that dared me to resist his invitation, if I could. I couldn't, and started unzipping my bridal gown as fast as my fingers could manage.

"I'll bring the strawberries!"

I heard the sound of water rushing out of the spout, and shivered, wondering what it would be like to make love under the stars, bubbles and jets surrounding us. I grinned, feeling like a very bad girl, and lifted up the silver tray of fruit. Beneath it was a plain, white envelope, the paper thick and beveled on the edges like a wedding invitation or an expensive thank you note.

I set the tray back down and picked it up. There was no name on it, so I turned it over and tore open the flap. There was a thick card inside with a typed message.

```
You have one month to come around,
reverse your stance on education reform.
Break your promise about youth center
funding,
    and you'll have more votes than you can count
come Election Day.

A friend guarantees it.
But, keep the fat untrimmed,
and you'll have made an enemy.
This marriage will be exposed
for the charade it is, and your reputation
will burn.

You'll never set foot in an office again,
much less as an elected official.

So what's it going to be, Jackson?
Do you want a thriving career, or a pet
project?
The choice is yours.

I'll be watching.
```

There was no signature, but the last line felt like one, heavy with meaning, hanging there like a disembodied stare, watching me even as I read what I now knew I should have left well alone.

Someone was threatening Jackson. Someone knew about the fake marriage and was using it to turn him away from his principles. Was using it to make him toothless, to cull away the heart of his platform. The very thing that made him different from the other candidates, candidates who didn't give a crap what happened to the community or the kids as long as they lined their pockets at the end of the day.

"Rose?"

Jackson appeared in the balcony doorway, stripped down to just his slacks, a flute of sparkling wine in one hand.

"Are you coming?"

I had to tell him. But if I did, I knew the night would be over. This moment of ours would shatter, and all that would be left was those watching eyes. Maybe it wouldn't hurt to keep it from him, just for tonight…

"Jackson," I said. "I… I think you'd better see this."

His brow furrowed, but he came inside, crossing the span between us in a few long strides. I handed him the note.

"It was under the tray."

He read, his expression changing from confusion to concern, then from concern to a neutral mask I recognized all too well. He wore this expression when he spoke to senators he didn't like or when he prepared to take the stage for a speech. It was the expression that masked his emotions. The false face that covered up the wildness inside of him. The mask that shielded the part of him I'd grown to love.

"Did you see anyone besides the waiter when I carried you inside? Anyone lingering in the hallway?"

I ran my hand over my forehead, trying to recall.

"I was too busy laughing, and… no, I don't know."

"Wait here."

He moved to the doorway in a flash, peering through the peephole in the door, before jerking open the locks and throwing it open. He disappeared into the hall, slamming the door behind him. I stood there, alone in my half-zipped wedding gown, staring down at the strawberries, now scattered across the tray, juice running like watered-down blood over the doily.

The door slammed again, and I jumped. Jackson's chest heaved, and he leaned against the door, his eyes shining, staring into nothing.

"What… was anyone there?"

My heart pounded, seeing him like this, anxiety filling my stomach with acid. I sat down, willing myself to calm down.

"No."

"What are you going to do?"

"I don't know."

He snapped the locks shut, wrestling briefly with the chain before jerking it into place. His tone was cool, but the tightness of his jaw betrayed him. He was freaking out just as much as I was. What did this mean to him? What must be going through his head right now?

He downed the champagne, still clutched in his hand, and threw the flute across the room. I yelped as it shattered against the entertainment unit, bits of glass sliding across the marble floor.

"Goodnight," he said.

He stripped his pants off, and stalked into the attached bedroom, closing the door behind him. I heard a gurgling noise, and realized the water on the balcony was still running.

Numbly, I pulled my dress off, and shucked my slip. I tip toed carefully around the glass shards on the floor, glancing toward the closed bedroom door, as if expecting Jackson to come out at any moment and say 'Just kidding! Everything's fine!'

It remained firmly shut.

On the balcony, the cool night air felt good against my skin. The tub was almost full, and I saw Jackson had poured some fragrant bubble bath into the water. It was frothy and iridescent in the light filtering out between the curtains of the suite, the champagne still in its bucket off to one side.

I snapped off the faucet and sunk into the water, hissing as the heat covered me. It was too hot since Jackson walked away from it, almost scalding, but right now, the pain felt good. Under the stars, wrapped in darkness, sitting there still in my white lace bra and panties, the contrast between hot and cold made me feel alive.

I reached for the champagne and took a swig right out of the bottle. Beads of condensation dripped down my wrist and onto my chest, the cold stinging me in a way that made me sigh.

I should have known things were going far too well. Too good to be true.

Every time in my life when something was going well, someone would come along and fuck it all up again. They'd hurt me, leave me, or take what I loved. Every time I thought I had something, someone would remind me that I grew up with nothing and that's what I'd die with—absolutely fuck all. No matter how hard I tried, whatever I wanted would always slip away.

Happiness was for other people. Not dirty little orphans like me.

And to make matters worse, someone wanted to ruin Jackson Pierce, taking him down, when he'd done nothing but try to make the world a little less shitty.

I sat back, draping my arms over the back of the tub and drank, looking out into the night, trying not to think about what new pain tomorrow would bring.

CHAPTER 20

I swam, my tail waving in the water gracefully, my naked body powerful, my muscles contracting pleasingly with each stroke as I cut through the clear, turquoise ocean water. My hair flowed all around me like seaweed, floating effortlessly in this new world, this beautiful, peaceful world where no one could harm me.

Fish swam past, rainbow colors glinting in the dappled sunlight filtering through the waves, and I smiled, bubbles rising from my lips. It felt so good not to need air, not to need land, not to need direction, in this ever-shifting universe of water and light.

I swam deeper, loving the way the currents felt against my skin, warm then cool, then floated, spinning around and around in the water, my fins sparkling below me, propelling me.

A shadow appeared above, blocking the light. Darkness moved toward me, and I shrugged back, away from it. The weeds below me jerked upward, grabbing me, biting into my tail and back, bunching my arms by my sides. I screamed, my voice muffled, gurgling. What I thought was just kelp was a net, a trap, closing around me, curling me in on myself until I couldn't move, couldn't struggle.

I screamed again and again, fighting impotently, the rope biting into my skin, cutting, burning, as I was dragged upwards, toward the shadow. Water burst around me, and air filled my chest. I gasped and choked, my lungs burning as human voices met my ears, jeering and laughing.

A large hand reached for me… and I shrieked with everything I had, expelling the last of my breath, my throat feeling like it would tear in two.

"Rose? Rose!"

I woke with a start, and for a moment, I didn't know where I was. I was damp, my skin sticking to leather, and Jackson stood over me, shaking me, his eyes wide.

"You were yelling in your sleep. I didn't mean to frighten you."

I sat up with a groan and looked around. Slowly, the events of last night came back to me. After finishing off the bottle of champagne by myself, I climbed out of the tub and hit the mini bar, drinking tiny bottles of vodka while watching infomercials and trying not to think any more.

I didn't know if Jackson wanted me in the room or not, so I stayed up, my wet lingerie rapidly cooling, chilling me, but I liked the way it felt. From the jabbing in the small of my back, I'd fallen asleep on the remote control.

My mouth felt like someone had stuffed it with cotton, and my head pounded dully. Everything was too bright, and there was a sour rumble in my stomach that made me groan.

"I'm okay. It was just a dream."

He sat down beside me, and I noticed he was dressed for the day in khaki slacks and a button-up shirt.

"Do you want to talk about it?"

It was already fading, bits flashing before me like… like dappled light over the water.

I'd dreamed of being a mermaid more times than I could count since my childhood, but this was the only time it ended like this. I'd loved the idea as a kid that I could step into the water, just like Darryl Hannah, and transform into something unique, something mystical and powerful and beautiful… and escape from this world into another where I was safe. Where no one I hated could find me. A world where I was special. A world where I belonged.

I suppose it was my version of the little boy who dreams of being told he's really a wizard or a prophesied One True King of a far off land.

Jackson's hand on my knee made me shiver.

"No, I'm okay."

He looked down at my bra, stuck to my erect nipples in a way that looked positively pornographic. I covered myself with one arm and drew a throw pillow into a hug over my crotch.

"What did you do last night?"

I sat up straighter, my body squeaking on the leather couch back. Maybe it was just the hangover, but I was in no mood to be judged, especially when I noticed broken glass twinkling near the patio.

"After you threw your little fit and slammed the door, I enjoyed a soak, that's all."

The look in his eyes instantly made me regret my words, but I set my jaw. I wouldn't apologize, not when he was pretending like nothing was wrong. Like he wasn't just as flustered as I was. Sitting there next to me like it was any other day, and he hadn't just been threatened.

That we hadn't just gotten married.

That we weren't both about to be exposed. Ruined. That my kids would never get help, either from him or me. Because I knew that I wouldn't get the money if Jackson was exposed. Why would I? The whole business arrangement would be moot. And even if he chose to give in to the demands and give up his reform policies, it would hurt the kids. The center was hanging on by a shoe string as is, and if he agreed to cut funding, they'd be ruined.

I didn't believe he would, not yet, but either way, I was pissed off and feeling ill. And it wasn't just the booze. The whole situation made my stomach churn.

Jackson stared me down, his mask firmly in place.

"You're right," he said. "My behavior last night was undignified. Inappropriate. I apologize, Rose. I didn't mean for you to sleep out here. I just needed… some time."

"Time to hide, you mean," I said.

Tears burned behind my eyes, but I held them in. What was wrong with me? I was ashamed of the way I was behaving, but I couldn't help it. Because behind the shame, I was angry. Angry at life. Angry at whoever was trying to ruin this. Angry at Jackson, because no matter what he did, I lost.

And so did he.

I couldn't stand it one more minute.

He didn't speak. Instead, he looked at me for one more minute, assessing me, looking through me, and then he stood, brushing off his slacks.

"Okay, then. Get dressed if you want breakfast. We leave for the wedding brunch in ten minutes."

I moaned and leaned back against the pillows. In all of the excitement from last night, I forgot about the brunch completely. The press would be there, along with a few of Jackson's most important financial supporters. I peeled myself off the couch and stumbled barefoot into the bathroom, wincing as a toe hit a sliver of glass. I blotted at the blood before I could track it everywhere, and did what I could with my time, washing my body with a hand towel and tugging a brush through my hair.

There was no time for anything fancy, so I just flattened down the bed head and covered up the bags under my eyes before jumping into a sundress and flats. A little lip gloss, and I looked like death warmed up. It was an improvement.

Jackson took my hand at the door, and nodded approvingly.

"Let's go, Mrs. Pierce."

I sighed as he led me out of the room, but before we left, I noticed a note for the housekeeper with another fifty and the words "sorry about the mess" written in Jackson's neat hand.

Some of my anger loosened as he closed the door behind us, and by the time we reached the elevator, I wondered if things were really as bleak as they seemed. If anyone would do the right thing, it was the man standing beside me. He always did, even when his world was falling apart.

The only problem was this seemed like an impossible situation.

I squeezed his hand and looked up into his eyes. He looked down at me and raised an eyebrow, but I wiped the confused look off his face with a kiss.

"I trust you," I said.

His lips quirked into a half smile.

"I trust you, too."

He kissed the back of my hand. When the elevator doors opened, I walked arm and arm with him to the brunch, and when I smiled for photos along the way, despite the fear and doubt I felt, it was as effortless as a fish gliding through water.

CHAPTER 21

That night, we sat, tucked into a private booth in one of the cities busiest clubs before heading back to the room. Jackson wanted to make damn sure we weren't overheard, while also making it look like we were enjoying our last night before we left on our honeymoon.

"We slipped up somewhere. It's as simple as that," Jackson said. "We have to figure out where, and plug the leak."

"Do you think it's just one person? I mean, if we screwed up, what if more people know, and just haven't said anything?"

Jackson glanced down at his smart phone again, pulling up the gossip blogs and flipping through them. I leaned over his shoulder.

"The media's just covering the wedding. Not a peep about a scandal, which would definitely be bigger than how much everyone loved your dress."

I put a hand to my lips. "They're talking about my dress?"

Jackson stared back at the screen and grunted his affirmation.

"Which is good news for us." He flipped from blog to blog, site to site. "Nothing but wedding this, wedding that. They loved the kids, by the way," he said, looking up. "Good move inviting them. That played really well."

He looked back down, reading TMZ's front page.

TIED TO HIM

I frowned at him. Of course I'd invite them to my wedding, even if it was the fake version. They were my world. Not everything about this was a media stunt, no matter what he thought.

"I'm thinking it's one person keeping a close watch. The obvious answer would be my opponent, Matt Ramsee, but I can't know for sure. And I certainly can't accuse him of trying to intimidate me. Not without proof."

"And not while he might have dirt on you," I muttered.

Jackson looked up.

"I mean, you couldn't confront him anyway, because he might leak any proof he does have out of spite, right?"

He ran his hand over his face and dropped his phone on the table.

"I can't believe this is happening. I've been such a fool… and now I've dragged you into this. Goddamn it."

I squeezed his leg in warning.

"Would you two like another round? Anything to nibble on?"

The server's bubbly voice cut through the noise of the crowded bar like a knife.

"Please, just some privacy," Jackson said, putting his arm around me.

She gave us a knowing smile. "Will do, Mr. Pierce."

I leaned on him as she made her way back to the bar.

"I never meant for you to be in the line of fire," he said, his lips brushing my hair.

"Don't worry about me," I said. "I don't have a reputation to ruin."

"You're not running for office, sure, but Rose, I know how much the teens at the center mean to you and how much they look up to you. I know you want to be a model for them. And now I've put that in jeopardy, too."

We sat in silence for a long moment, each of us lost in thought. Across the bar was a mirror, and when the crowd shifted, for one moment, I saw us together, his arm draped around me, my head on his shoulder.

We look like a real couple.

How had anyone found us out? We'd been so careful, not even Mr. Pierce's driver knew what we were up to. That just left the lawyer, Jackson himself, and the woman who ran his campaign, but they had too much to lose to betray him like that.

"Selfish."

He spit it like a curse word, and leaned back with a sigh.

"I'm so goddamn selfish, sometimes. I hate that about myself."

"What? How can you think that?"

He shook his head. "I just want too many things. I hurt my father when I turned down the job of running his company because I wanted to live my own life. I hurt my brother because he had to take the brunt of father's anger after that. I wanted to run my way, on my platform, and… I wanted to be with someone…"

His voice trailed off, and he frowned down at the table.

"You wanted to be with someone you could love your way, and it got you in trouble."

He sighed.

"First the rumors, and now I'm hurting you, too, Rose. So fucking selfish."

"Stop it," I said.

The snap in my tone made his eyes widen. He pulled his arm away.

"What?"

"I said stop it, Jackson. It's not selfish to want to pursue your own goals instead of being forced into a life you never asked for. It's not goddamn selfish to be able to be yourself with a woman for five minutes, instead of being scrutinized and judged and… I don't know how you even stand it. I would go nuts if I put that kind of pressure on myself. So just… shut up and stop giving yourself a beating you don't deserve. You can hate yourself later if you do something actually selfish, I promise, but for now, you're not helping, and you're driving me up the wall."

He stared at me, and for a moment, I thought I'd gone too far. He was going to leave. Walk away in a cool huff. But just when I thought he'd snap, he did something I didn't expect.

He laughed. A big, belly laugh of pure, childish delight, his eyes sparkling with surprise.

"What's so funny?"

I folded my arms over my chest. This was weird. I didn't get it, and I didn't like it.

"N-no," he laughed again, and held his side, trying to catch his breath. "No one's ever yelled at me like that before."

It was my turn to stare.

"It was great. I always wanted someone to tell me off when I was being stupid or bullheaded, but no one ever did."

He put a hand on my thigh under the table.

"I always thought it would be a good sign if someone cared enough about me to call me out once in a while."

I laughed, shaking my head in disbelief.

"You're not making any sense."

"I heard a saying once that's always stuck with me. The opposite of love isn't anger or hate. It's apathy."

I looked away, feeling the impact of his words like a punch in the gut. I'd felt the sting of apathy only too many times in my life —the apathy of people charged with caring for me, when all I wanted was to be safe. To be loved. Instead, I was ignored. Abandoned. Traded away to home after home like a piece of junk nobody wanted.

I leaned against him again, and his hand squeezed my thigh. We sat like that for a long while, just being together, my head spinning as I wondered what on earth we were going to do next.

CHAPTER 22

"Jackson? I didn't expect to hear from you until after the honeymoon? She wear you out already?"

I rubbed a hand over my forehead at the sound of Max's voice through the phone. My little brother. Always the comedian.

"Max, I need you to listen right now. Can you and Lucy meet me in an hour? I… I need your help."

I knew Max and his girlfriend Lucy had recently faced down some trouble, and they'd dealt with their blackmailers together. If anyone could advise me now, it would be them.

"You need me? Well… I guess there is a first time for everything," he said.

"Can you do it or not?" I sighed.

There was a silence on the other end of the line.

"Where?"

"My hotel. Presidential Suite."

"See you in an hour, brother."

The line went dead.

I sat back against the pillows on the bed, listening to the sound of Rose splashing in the shower. The last thing I wanted was a repeat of last night. I needed a plan, some kind of forward momentum on this thing, or I'd be the same pain in the ass I'd been the night before. She didn't deserve that. None of this was her fault, but here she was, in the middle of it. The last thing she needed was me shutting her out.

But I couldn't relax, couldn't even think, when something was hanging over my head, especially something like this. I'd been threatened once before in my life, by a bully I'd drag-raced back in my wilder days growing up with Max. I won his car, but he couldn't accept the humiliation. He and two of his friends beat me half to death that day, but my brother came to my rescue, offering up another race, another car, a chance for him to save face.

I still had a small scar on my lower back where they'd kicked me so badly I needed stitches, but the lingering hurt was knowing I couldn't protect myself. That my younger brother had to bail me out.

That day, I promised myself that would never happen again.

But here I was again. Calling Maxwell. Asking for a favor, when there was nothing I could do to protect myself from this new threat. This new bully.

But if there was one thing I learned during my time as a D.A., it was that sometimes you had to make the hard choices in order to do the right thing, and sometimes that hard choice meant putting your ego aside.

I needed to find out what was going on, needed to seek out the blackmailer and find a solution to all of this that didn't involve my humiliation or me caving into their demands. But I couldn't stay here and look into it myself. If Rose and I didn't get on a plane to our honeymoon destination tomorrow, the marriage would look suspicious to more than just one unscrupulous asshole. And that was one thing I couldn't allow to happen.

Rose's voice came to me, floating on a curl of steam under the bathroom door, singing an old bluegrass hymn. My heart warmed hearing it, thinking of her in there, my friend, hopefully still my lover... the woman who unexpectedly turned my world upside down.

The thought of her standing naked under the running water, rivulets running down her perfect breasts, steam beading glistening droplets on her round ass as she washed herself, soaping her curves before her hand parted those firm thighs...

The door opened with a bang, and she emerged, a towel around her waist, whistling softly. She smiled sadly at me, then her eyes drifted lower, to the erection now straining my khaki pants. I coughed and shifted, trying to cover it, but it was too late.

"And just what were you thinking about?"

"You."

My father always said, honest was the best policy.

"Oh, really."

She waltzed over to me, her short hair clinging to her neck, the cleavage visible just above the towel making my cock jump in my pants.

"What about me?"

I jerked the towel off her body with one quick motion, and she squealed as her wet skin hit the cool air. I gathered her onto my lap until she straddled me, slippery and naked and absolutely gorgeous.

"Everything," I growled.

I thrust upward, grinding against her, and she moaned, biting her lip. I kissed her hard, tasting the droplets from her hair on my tongue. I rolled her over, pinning her to the bed and bit first one hard nipple, then the other, groaning as they stiffened against my lips.

"We only have an hour before guest arrive."

She wrapped her arms around me, her small hands gripping my ass.

"Then what are you waiting for?"

The zipper rasped downward on my pants, and she gripped me hard. I growled, bucking up into her hand, and ripped my shirt up over my head.

And for thirty minutes, my troubles slipped away as I buried myself in Rose's hot, tight body, loving her so fiercely that my mind didn't have room for anything else, wanting her so much it frightened me.

When she cried out beneath me, her nails raking my back, a tear slid down my cheek. I buried my face in her neck and thrust again and again, trying to make the moment last as long as possible, chasing away the hollow feeling inside of me as I long as I could. Like all good things, it eventually came to an end. But this time, the end was beautiful.

Just like Rose. Just like every little thing about her.

"Let me get this straight," Lucy said, her red curls wild around her face. "Someone's fucking blackmailing you?"

Max hid a grin beneath his hand and cleared his throat. He'd told me Lucy swore like a sailor when she got excited, but hearing it in person was something else. I exchanged a glance with Rose, and could tell by her expression she felt the same way I did. Max must have done something right to keep a firecracker like Lucy on his side.

"Pretty much," I said.

"And you're telling me that you and Rose aren't really…?"

"I'm helping your brother because I believe in him," Rose said. "We all have a past, we've all done things that other people may disagree with, but that doesn't define us as people."

Max nodded, his brow furrowed, watching Rose carefully.

"You know about the Club?"

"I do, and I don't give a damn about that. People should be free to be themselves, and it doesn't goddamn matter what consenting adults get up to behind closed doors. What matters is what you do in the daylight. How kind you are to other people. What actions you take to make this world a better place for people who don't have your advantages in life. That's what defines a person. Not their goddamn sex lives."

"A-fucking-men," said Lucy, crossing her arms. "People are more than the sum of their genitals slapping together with other people's genitals."

There was a moment of shocked silence, then Rose cracked up, covering her mouth with her hand.

"Exactly!"

Tears leaked from her eyes, and soon Lucy was laughing with her, bringing Max and I along. We laughed long and hard, letting off the steam that had built up inside of us, the tension poisoning us, seeking release. When we finally calmed down, I wiped tears from my own eyes and shook my head, trying to clear it.

As absurd as this was, it was no joke. We had to come together on a solution, or Rose and I were in serious trouble.

"Okay, okay," Max said, sitting up straighter. "So you're covering for him. I get it. It's fine. I forgive you both for lying to me," he said, raising an eyebrow at me.

I shrugged, and he continued.

"So someone found out, and now they're coming after you?"

"I'm afraid so."

I pushed the note across the table, and watched as my they read it together, Max looking over Lucy's shoulder. Their eyes widened at the same time, and both of them swore under their breath. Max whistled low and pushed it back.

"Any idea what you're going to do?"

"That's why I called you here. Both of you. We need eyes and ears on the ground trying to figure out who might know about us, and who would benefit from me flipping my views. We can't cancel the honeymoon trip and investigate ourselves, or it will just look worse, but there's no time to waste."

"You want us to turn over some rocks for you?"

"I know it's a lot to ask," I said, but Max shook his head, gesturing for me to continue. "We suspect it may be someone in Matt Ramsee's campaign. He has the most to gain from me flip-flopping, after all. Especially since my education platform is what sets us apart for the women and minority voters."

Lucy turned to Max. "Do you know anyone in local politics?"

"No, but I know who might."

He gave Lucy a knowing glance, and she nodded.

"Right. If he can handle that side of it, you and I can stake out Jackson's campaign headquarters."

"Wait, my headquarters?"

Suddenly, I felt like these two were talking past me. Who were they calling for a favor? What about my headquarters?

"Well, obviously you have a leak, right? If Ramsee's team is behind it, they probably are getting their info from someone inside your operation, don't you think?"

Lucy stared at me with an exasperated look on her face.

"I… I suppose that's true, but I handpicked everyone myself. No one would betray me like that. Besides, only two people know, aside from Rose, that is."

"The lawyer and his campaign manager," Rose said.

"Neither of them have anything to gain from fucking me over!"

All eyes turned to me.

"Ken, of all people knows that if he betrays my confidence, I'll have him disbarred. He'd never work again. And as for Lisa, she's the one who came up with this idea, for Christ's sake. She's been covering my ass on this. Her reputation is staked upon her running winning campaigns. If this got out, her career would be ruined just as much as mine."

"Maybe it's not them, then. Maybe someone overheard something when Lisa told you. Saw something. It could be one of the poll workers for all we know," Max said.

I took a deep breath, trying to calm down. To think clearly.

"All we know for sure is that someone knows something, or at least thinks they do. And they're connected enough to make trouble for me."

"We'll check it out," Max said. "I can say I'm holding down the fort while you're on your honeymoon. I am your brother, after all," he said, beaming. "Besides, I've been wanting to take a vacation from the company for awhile. It will be a nice change of pace."

"This isn't exactly going to be a vacation, Max," I said, sighing. "This is my life's work on the line."

"I know! It's exciting. I've always wanted to play spy."

"Bond," Lucy said, giggling. "Max Bond."

This was getting out of hand.

"Maybe this was a bad idea. I could always say I'm ill, or that I have to prepare for the rally. It is the day after our return flight…"

"Jackson," Max said, suddenly serious. "We've got your back on this, I promise. We won't let you down."

Lucy reached across the table and gave Rose's hand a squeeze. Rose startled, then squeezed back, a look of relief crossing her face. That, more than anything, made me finally relax.

"Thank you both," I said. "I mean it."

"Anything. You're family."

Max stood and clapped me on the shoulder, then pulled me into a tight hug. I hesitated, then put my arms around him, hugging him back, savoring this rare moment. When we finally broke apart, I hugged Lucy, too.

"Alright. We leave tomorrow morning at 8 a.m. and we'll be gone all week. It's a long flight, but I'll call you as soon as we get in. Keep me updated, okay? Call me every day. I want to be in the know if you find anything."

"Yeah, yeah, we know you're a control freak. You established that long ago."

I gave Max a warning look, and he raised his hands, shrugging.

"What? I'll call. I'll call!"

"It'll all be okay," Lucy said, pulling Rose into a hug. "We have friends in high places. We'll figure a way out of this before you even know it."

"Thank you," Rose said, her cheeks coloring.

Maybe she had as hard a time letting go as I did.

We said our goodbyes and got packing. Our flight would be Rose's first time flying first class, but it was a redeye and we had to hurry. Despite everything, all of the stress, all of the dread over what might be, I wanted her to enjoy this trip. I hadn't told her where we were going, but I'd chosen it specifically for her.

Because, despite this starting out as strictly business, I knew I was falling fast, and that thought, more than anything, made me hopeful that everything would be alright in the end. It had to be.

Rose Turner was not just any woman. She was the kind of woman I knew I couldn't let get away. I just hoped she felt the same way about me.

CHAPTER 23

I rolled my eyes when Jackson said he wanted me to cover them, walking off the plane. I'd slept through the landing, and still had no idea where we were, although the air when we reached the door was warm and pleasantly humid.

First class had been ridiculous. Hot towels, free wine, gourmet snacks, cold towels, free champagne, seats that lay flat like beds, and more wine… it was almost as if the crew purposefully tried to overindulge you into a stupor so you'd leave them alone, and boy, did it work.

"Trust me, Rose," Jackson said, his presence behind me a comfort. "I want to surprise you. Indulge me."

I sighed dramatically, but I couldn't hide my smile.

"I suppose I can do that."

He put his large hand over my eyes, and carefully guided me off the plane, through the airport, and into a waiting car. When he finally removed his hand, I looked around quickly, greedy for information. We were in the backseat of a town car with tinted windows and a partition, blocking the front from view. I raised an eyebrow at him.

"You're kidding me. I still can't know?"

"Wait for it," he said.

He leaned back, smirking at me with his arm around my shoulder. He was obviously enjoying this. But, hey, if he wanted to be Mr. Mysterious, I'd let him. This trip was on his dime, after all.

The car rolled away from the curb, and I had a moment of panic.

"Did we just forget our bags?"

"Rose, relax," he said. "They'll be waiting for us at the hotel."

I sat back, shaking my head. He'd thought of everything, of course. I was never going to get used to this kind of life, where your assistant just arranged for your bags to be picked up for you. It was so alien, but I had to admit, not a bad way to travel.

We drove in a comfortable silence, me still waking up, Jackson holding me close in a way that made me feel like we really were newly weds, and couldn't keep our hands off one another. The way my stomach did a flip when he caressed my arm certainly helped the illusion. I knew I had to be careful, but it was just so goddamn hard to stay rational around him.

The way he'd taken me on the bed last night after my shower made my toes curl just thinking about it. I looked up at him and saw him watching me, a smile on his lips.

"What?"

"Nothing, Mrs. Pierce," he said.

He kissed me softly, and I sighed, all of my resolve to keep my feelings in check slipping away, like water through my clenched hand.

"Nothing at all."

When we pulled up at our destination, I had no idea what to expect. We were definitely somewhere hot and sunny, I knew that much from the air conditioning blowing on me, and that brief sweaty feel of the air on the way from the plane to the car. Mexico, maybe? Hawaii?

I'd never been to either. Hell, I'd never been out of the continental U.S. of A. I was so excited for the reveal, I voluntarily closed my eyes before Jackson could demand it. He held my hand and helped me out of the car.

A chorus of children's voices greeted me, and I jumped about a mile. My eyes flew open, and I covered my mouth as kids ran up to us, laughing and yelling. My laughter joined theirs.

"Welcome to Jamaica!"

A friendly woman in a navy dress greeted us, holding out her hand. Kids were everywhere, tugging on the hem of my tank top, and staring up at Jackson with curious eyes.

We shook her hand, me in a state of shocked surprise, and Jackson grinning beside me like it was Christmas morning.

"Mr. Pierce said you'd be visiting us today," the woman said. "We're so delighted. My name is Shanice, and I'm so happy to show you our facility here."

I glanced up at the building behind us, a whitewashed building made of concrete blocks. A sign read "Food for the Poor: Drop Off Center." Numbly, I shook the woman's hand, mouthing a greeting. I don't know what I expected when Jackson said he planned this trip just for me, but this was a huge surprise.

Jackson took my hand and led me along, following Shanice as she took us inside. I glanced back, smiling as the children ran and played in the grassy field surrounding the center, scaring chickens and kicking a ball around that looked like it had seen better days.

"We take donations here, either in school supplies, food items or cash, and distribute them to the locals in need."

Shanice pointed to a collection room where young men and women sorted goods. They looked up and waved, and I waved back as I walked past.

"There are sites like this one all over the Caribbean, and we could always use more help, which is why we really appreciate you two coming down. So far, we've been blessed enough to sponsor twenty one orphanages just in Jamaica, which is a huge accomplishment."

She turned to me and took my hand in hers, patting me like she was a relative, instead of a stranger.

"Mr. Pierce told me over the phone that you work with homeless and foster children," she said. "Come take a look at our kids. I know they'll make you smile."

She took us into a backroom where people prepared boxes of dry food and produce for distribution. Beside their work table was a giant bulletin board with polaroids of children of all ages, some holding up lunch pails and grinning widely, and some sitting in a school room in matching uniforms, the girls with ribbons in their braids and the boys looking smart in their ties.

"Our school hunger program feeds over 150,000 children just on our island, thanks to donations like yours."

I glanced up at Jackson, but he was already thanking our host for her service to the community and moving on to shake the hands of the other workers. I followed suit, admiring their work and asking questions, waiting to admit my surprise until Jackson and I were alone.

When we left a half hour later, the kids waved goodbye, and I laughed and waved, happy that they had a place like this looking after them.

"What's all that about?" I said once we were tucked back in the car.

"Well," he said. "Remember how I told you I wanted this vacation to be a surprise just for you?"

"Yes?"

"I wanted to pamper you, give you a taste of real luxury, but I knew you couldn't enjoy it unless I did something to help you relax about the cost."

I raised an eyebrow. He really did know me, didn't he? I already felt guilty enough about the plane tickets, one of which cost more than a month's rent.

"So, I did something to fix that," he said, smiling.

The edges of his dark eyes crinkled in a way that made me smile back.

"For every dollar you let me spend on you during this honeymoon, I'll match a dollar and donate it to this charity. I already cut them a check matching the cost of the accommodations and airfare, and now it's up to you to really rack up that bill."

He winked at me, laughing at my stunned expression.

"But... I can't... you can't... How much money are you spending?"

"Don't feel guilty about me, too, Rose. Do you know how much I made just in capital gains last year?"

I shook my head, afraid of the answer.

"Let's just say it's more than a thousand times what we'll pay for this trip, even if you get a hot stone massage twice a day every day. I can more than afford it."

A noise halfway between a squeal and a cough escaped my lips.

"Let me give you this gift," he said.

He rubbed my knee, his touch making my body heat.

"We have to honeymoon anyway, but... I want to make you happy, Rose."

I didn't know what to say. No one had ever done anything so kind for me, or understood what I needed so much. Instead of talking, I reached for him, pulling his head down to mine and kissed him hard, my heart full to bursting.

This man was something special. No matter what happened, I'd never forget this moment, this gift. This kiss with the man I knew I was falling in love with more and more each minute I spent by his side.

"Welcome to our bungalow. Do you like it?"

I ran inside, feeling like a kid in a candy shop. The 'bungalow' was actually a gigantic suite, built like a tropical hut out over the lagoon, standing half on it's own piece of tropical island and half on stilts disappearing beneath the turquoise water. The inside was wood paneled and decorated tastefully with local art, shells, and flowing white curtains. It was gorgeous.

I checked out the bathroom, and gasped when I saw the massive shower.

"There's a window!"

I pointed downward, and felt Jackson behind me. He chuckled and placed his hands on my shoulders.

"The shower and the bedroom floor both have glass panels overlooking the lagoon. It feels like you're walking on water, or snorkeling from the comfort of your bedside."

A school of brightly-colored fish swam by, and I did a little dance of excitement. I'd never seen anything so awesome in my life.

"You've got to be kidding me!"

"And there's a hot tub on the deck overlooking the water," he said. "Our privacy is guaranteed."

His voice was low now, husky, and I felt him pressing against me.

"That's why I booked this particular bungalow. Not only is it the best, but this part of the lagoon is ours alone, the jungle cutting us off from view. We could swim naked if we wanted..."

His hands roamed over me, moving down my arms, then encircling me, cupping and squeezing my breasts. I sighed and leaned back, going limp against him, reaching up and circling my arm around his neck, giving him full access to my body.

This was all so intoxicating. The room, the water, the heart of the man behind me, a man who I burned for whenever he touched me.

He kissed my earlobe, then suckled it gently, making me squirm against him. His hardness rubbed between my cheeks, hot and needy, and I reached back to stroke him. He growled against my neck.

Just then, there was a knock at the door.

"Room service for Mr. and Mrs. Pierce."

Jackson swore and held me tight for one moment, before moving back and adjusting himself. He opened the door to the bungalow, his eyes flashing dangerously.

"Your brunch, Sir, as requested, and of course, complimentary champagne for the newlyweds. Please let us know if you have any special requests—We'd love to make this trip unforgettable in any way we can."

Jackson rolled the cart into the room and practically strong-armed the young man out the door, pressing money into his hand before he could protest.

"You timed this so we could eat after you took me to see the charity," I said, impressed.

He nodded, looking distracted.

"Oh, Jackson." I threw my arms around him. "You're amazing. I mean, I know that it's... that we're not..."

"Stop."

He grabbed me, sweeping me off my feet. I screamed, then laughed as he took me onto the wooden patio floating over the lagoon, a wooden ladder leading down into the water. A hot tub as big as a small swimming pool was set down into it, glass on the bottom, so we felt like we were floating, swimming even as we relaxed.

"Don't say anything else, Rose. Brunch can wait. Talk can wait. But I can't wait any longer."

He yanked my top up over my head, and I gasped. My shorts followed, hitting the deck before I could even agree with him, my bra clasp ripping free of the fabric as he tore it off my body. My panties didn't even stand a chance, and soon, I stood there naked, shocked, and already so wet I felt like I'd taken a swim in the lagoon.

The ferocious way he wanted me made me burn like nothing else. I reached for him, but he batted my hands away.

"No," he barked. "Stand with your hands behind your back, Rose. I want to look at you."

Wide-eyed, I did as he asked.

He undid his shirt slowly, my eyes following his motions, caressing his tightly muscled chest and stomach with my gaze. I felt his eyes on me at the same time, the moment stretching out, making me feel vulnerable, yet somehow, bold, standing naked and proud before him, not daring cover myself, hands behind me, ready for whatever he wanted, whatever he had in store.

A half smile twisted my lips. I'd never felt that way before, but somehow this man brought out a confidence in me I never knew I had. When he looked at me like this, I knew I was beautiful, and so much more.

I was intoxicating.

He lowered his pants, and I licked my lips when I saw his gorgeous cock spring free from the fabric. He held himself, stroking his shaft as he took his fill, drinking in my body, eyes traveling over the nape of my neck down to my nipples, pebbling in the morning breeze, over the gentle swell of my hips and down to my sex, which I knew was gleaming with arousal.

All because of him.

"Beautiful," he said. "So fucking beautiful."

It was hard to stand still, watching him touch himself like that, unashamed, totally uninhibited, and so sexy it made me blush. But I couldn't look away.

He sat on the edge of the hot tub, putting his feet in the water and sighing at the temperature.

"Get in," he said. "Come to me."

"Yes, Sir."

His grin was feral, his gaze ravenous as I got into the water, hissing at the change in sensation between the warm island air and the heat of the tub. It was just right, relaxing my muscles, making the air seem cooler, more inviting. I walked over to him, eyeing his lap, now just below eye-level.

"Keep your hands behind your back. Do you think you can do that?"

"Yes, Sir."

"Because you'll need to trust me. And if you don't keep them there, I'll have to tie you, understood?"

I nodded and bit my lip. What did he want me to do?

"Now," he said, spreading his legs wide, his cock pointing up at me like a spear. "Suck me, Rose."

I sucked in a breath. He was so beautiful, holding the base of his shaft toward my lips, the tip already glistening with a bead of cum, hard and throbbing for me.

"Yes, Sir," I breathed.

He groaned at my words, and wound a hand in my hair, holding me tight. It wasn't uncomfortable the way he held me, but his total control made me moan as he helped me lower my mouth to him, supporting me as I bent, hands clasped firmly behind my back.

When my tongue hit the head, licking up his salty sweetness, he let out a hard breath, whimpering. I grinned, loving that I was driving him wild, that it was my turn to take him, to own his pleasure, even though he was the one dominating me. The idea that I could submit to him while also teasing him, was almost too much.

I wrapped my lips around him slowly and looked up into his eyes, licking softly with my tongue as I took him in. His eyes were half-lidded, his lips parted as he watched me taste him. He bucked upward, holding my head firmly as he pushed himself inside me, making me take more of him in. I relaxed around him, letting him steady me, licking the bottom of his shaft with relish, suckling hard.

He smelled like soap and just a hint of musky male sweat, the taste of him filling my senses. I groaned around him as I pulled back, then bobbed back down, loving the way he filled me, even this way. Jackson groaned when I pulled back again and sucked hard on the spot just beneath the head.

"Fuck," he said. "God, that's good."

I chuckled and sucked him in again, trying to take as much as possible, loosening my throat, surprised at how relaxing it was being held this way, trusting him not to let me topple over, bound by my obedience to him. By my need to please him. To make him say my name when he finally found his release.

I picked up the pace now, letting him aid the rhythm, pushing and pulling in time with my motions, helping my head up and down as he fed me his cock, inch by inch, again and again.

I was lost in the moment, looking up at him beneath my lashes as he savored me and I savored him, his breathing ragged above me, his abs tensing as I sucked and licked along his length.

"Enough," he said, his voice strained.

He tugged my hair, and I released him with one parting lick, pouting.

"I want to taste you," I said.

"Well I want to fuck you until you cum all over my cock with that tight little pussy of yours."

His hand wrapped lightly around my throat, his thumb caressing the hollow in a way that made me shiver, despite the warmth of the tub. My core throbbed, aching for him, and I mewled, begging wordlessly for him to make good on his words.

He flipped me around and pressed me against the curved edge of the tub, one hand still holding my neck, the pressure just enough to send a thrill of fear through me, mingling with my arousal, but light enough where I knew he was taking care not to hurt me.

He jerked my hair, and I cried out. His teeth rasped against my neck, his body pressed aggressively against mine.

"Tell me," he said, "what you want."

He bit my earlobe, and I shuddered in his arms, captive, and so turned on my whole body ached.

"I… want you to fuck me…"

He jerked my hair again, and pinched my breasts with his other hand until I whimpered, writhing against him.

"I want you to fuck me, what?"

"Sir!" I said, my eyes watering. "I want you to fuck me, Sir!"

With an animal growl, he tightened his grip on my hair, his other hand snaking between my legs, testing my wetness. I moaned when he touched me, the rough pads of his fingers caressing my slick folds. When I felt him between my legs, his long, hot sex seeking my entrance, I arched my back, pushing back toward him, needing him, desperate to feel him inside me.

He thrust into me in one rough motion, and I cried out, gripping the edge of the tub, water splashing around me. Jackson grunted behind me, and applied pressure to the fist full of hair, making my scalp sting as he pulled out slowly, then slammed home, ramming into me up to the hilt.

The sweet touch of pain made the feel of him stretching me, filling me completely, even more overwhelming. I wailed as he moved inside of me, the friction intense with my legs so close together. He held my throat again with his open palm, making me arch my pack even more as he pumped into me again and again, making me gasp against his touch.

His breathe was in my ear, his voice ragged as he whispered to me, filling my mind as he filled my body, his words filthy, base, raw, so much different from the Jackson he showed to the world. This was the Jackson only I could see, and only like this, when both of us were stripped down, bound together in passion, the smell of sex surrounding us. Both of us bared down to the bone.

And just then, as I felt myself rising, my mind spinning to the beat of his words, matching the rhythm of our breath, his body pistoning into my own, I wondered if that's how he saw me, too, when I submitted to him, when I let my reserve fall away and just… trusted. Was I a different Rose? Was this the real me, carnal and open and… free?

I screamed as I came, and he pulled my hair hard, sending me higher as my pleasure surged through me, pumping through my veins like sheer adrenaline, sheer ecstasy, sheer bliss as I felt him swell, too, cumming inside me like a jolt of electrical current.

"Rose," he cried. "Rose…"

And his lips were on me, kissing my neck, sucking, licking as I convulsed again and again, milking his cock, wanting all he had to give and more, draining him dry as I pushed back against him, writhing and moaning like an animal.

We moved together for a long while, slowly grinding, until finally, he lay limp over my back, his arms on either side of me as we panted against the side of the tub, him still inside of me, joined to me, loving me.

When he slipped out of me, I sighed, missing him, but then he turned me around and kissed me so tenderly, I wanted to cry. He kissed me and kissed me, cupping my face, stealing my breath away all over again, and I wondered if I heard words in those kisses, things he couldn't say, but wanted me to know.

Words that whispered… I love you.

CHAPTER 24

"Chase Drake knows someone in his campaign? Ah, from his university. Perfect. Can he…? Yes, of course. Do it."

I towel dried my hair, listening intently to the phone conversation happening just feet away in the living room. Fish swam by beneath my feet in the marble shower, and I traced their path with my toe, squeaking softly on the wet glass.

I'd dreamed again last night about gliding through the water, cutting through it effortlessly with my fins. This time, though, I was alone. There was no shadow overhead. No threat ready to pull me out of the water and capture me. It was peaceful. I'd woken more refreshed than I'd felt in days.

"And how about you two? Lucy did what?"

There was a heavy pause.

"You've got someone special on your hands there, Max." A low chuckle. "But nothing on your end?"

Jackson sighed, and I pictured him running a hand over his forehead, with that defensive, neutral look of his.

"I understand. Keep your ear to the ground. And Max? Thank you. Thank you both."

Silence fell. I wrapped myself in one of the resort's soft terry cloth robes and padded into the room. Jackson leaned back on the sofa, staring out at the sunset, his eyes far away. I sat next to him and rested my hand on his thigh.

"Anything?"

He rested his head on his hand, his elbow on the edge of the couch.

"Max has a friend, Chase Drake, who knows someone high up in Ramsee's campaign. It sounds like Chase's going to connect with him and feel out what he's heard about the wedding. Max has been in my office all day saying he's covering my meetings, and Lucy took all the women out to lunch."

I smiled, thinking of the way Lucy reassured me before I walked down the aisle, and the outrage sparkling in her eyes when she heard Jackson was being blackmailed. There was something about her I instantly liked. I just hoped the office women would, too. That they'd open up to her.

"Max said when they came back, she'd got them all signed up to do a book club with her."

I laughed. "Wow. She moves fast."

"No kidding. They're going to be getting together for the first time this week, so hopefully we'll have some gossip collected by one of those three before we get back in town."

"Well, good. It's a start, and that's better than nothing, right?"

"Right," he said, but his eyes were still distant, still lost in thought.

"We'll figure it out."

He pulled me close, and for a while, we just sat together, watching the sunset streak the sky with a riot of color, fuscia and copper and gold blending together over the waves. The patio doors stood open, and the sea breeze washed over us. We sat until darkness fell, together, waiting for the tide to shift.

We made love like people who knew their time together was ending, each time an experience that left my body and heart aching together, sweetly hurting from wanting more and knowing I may never get it.

Jackson and Max spoke each night, and each night the news was more of the same. Chase's contact seemed convinced that Jackson was one lucky guy, honeymooning, and his staff was even luckier, taking a break from prepping appearances while he was gone. Apparently, he spent the entire phone call with Chase complaining about Ramsee the Slave Driver, after they'd done their catching up. There wasn't a single mention of any rumors about Jackson, believed or otherwise.

Max had even less luck sniffing out a mole in the campaign office, and instead worked with Lisa on the details for the speech Jackson was giving when he got back. He laughed with the interns at the phone bank and drank with the PR people, and came away with nothing but well wishes and some ribald comments about me that Jackson wouldn't repeat.

Lucy's book club had a successful first meeting, with almost all the women in the office showing up, clutching their copies of The Secretary: A Journey With Hilary Clinton. They ate and drank plenty of prosecco, but all that came out was that Jan in legal was cheating on her husband with her son's college roommate. There wasn't a peep about the wedding, except to say that the reception was great, but there could have been more seating by the dance floor.

Jackson and I spent the days distracting one another as best we could.

When we weren't in one another's arms, we got couples' massages and ate gourmet meals prepared by a private chef. He took me snorkeling all over the island, taking helicopter rides to remote beaches. I agreed after he reminded me he'd match the cost to the charity, and had one of the best times of my life, flying over the scenery, taking in the glint of waves crashing against the cliffs and caressing the sandy beaches.

My first time in the snorkel mask, I panicked, but Jackson held my hand until my breathing calmed, and I realized I was going to live. I could trust the snorkel and breath while holding my head underwater. I laughed when I realized I was floating, breathing freely, the sound echoing oddly in my mask.

Jackson gestured ahead and kicked his flippers, pulling my hand so I'd follow. I kicked along beside him, and soon found myself gliding effortlessly through the crystalline water, giggling like an idiot through my mouthpiece, and not giving a damn.

A whole underwater world unfolded beneath me, coral structures jutting upward like candy castles, breathtaking anemones wafting in the current like they were waving in greeting. Fish darted around and between us, their colors brilliant and exotic, and for the first time in my life, I felt like a dream of mine had come true.

In those hours we spent swimming beneath the waves, I was a mermaid, and no can tell me differently.

Now all I needed was to fight crime in Gotham, and I could die happy.

I smiled at the thought. Finally, I had a joy I could hold onto, something that was mine. A dream captured that I'd remember always, and no one could take it away from me. It was a very good feeling.

When we got back to the resort on the last night of our honeymoon, I was pleasantly worn out, my thighs tingling from kicking all day, and my stomach growling. Candles burned on the patio, and I noticed a table set for two near the hot tub, right on the edge of the railing, water lapping just a few feet down in the lagoon. The stars shone overhead, the night clear and quiet.

Wine chilled in a bucket next to an exquisite-looking lobster dish. I turned around, and saw Jackson, leaning against the patio door, watching me with a half smile on his face.

"Thank you," I said.

"What for?"

"For this. All of this."

I turned away, looking out over the water, trying to hold back the tears welling up, unwanted.

"Rose?"

He was there in the space of a breath, pulling me to him. I clutched his shirt and pressed my face to his shoulder.

"What's wrong?"

"Nothing," I said, my voice muffled. "Nothing's wrong... It's just..."

He pulled back and tilted my chin up, drawing my eyes to his.

"Just what?"

"I just never expected this. You're so kind to me. You didn't have to be, but you are, and I don't know how to thank you… for the best week of my life."

He pulled me close, holding me, rocking slowly with me almost like we were dancing.

"Don't say anything. Just… enjoy it. I want you to enjoy it. It makes me happy to see you trying things. To have you accepting what I have to give. It's wonderful to see things through your eyes," he said. "Better."

I looked up at him, confused.

"I've been all over the world, Rose. I've stayed in six star hotels on five continents, and eaten food prepared by the finest chefs. But it all pales compared to watching your face when you realized your plane seat folds all the way back. To watching you try a fine champagne. To watching you caressing the pillowcase like it's the softest thing you've ever felt."

"It is," I muttered, suddenly embarrassed.

"I know," he said, smiling. "I'm saying this badly, but… making you happy is my luxury, Rose. To be honest, this week is the best week of my life, too. You've given me something money can't buy."

He kissed my forehead, and I sighed.

"I'll never forget it."

We looked at one another a long moment, the breeze over the lagoon making the candlelight flicker, each of us looking overwhelmed, neither of us knowing what to say. Finally, Jackson pulled out my chair for me and poured the wine.

"Have you ever had lobster tail before, Rose?"

"No, Jackson. I haven't."

He smiled, watching me closely as I took my first bite.

CHAPTER 25

Just like waking from a beautiful dream, eventually the day of our return dawned, sunlight falling over the sheets where we lay tangled together. We rose and packed in silence, and after Jackson handed a check so large it made my eyes water over to a disbelieving Sharice, we boarded our plane and headed back to the real world.

During the flight, Jackson was quiet, working on the speech for his rally coming up the next day. I leaned over, resting my chin on his shoulder, reading what he had so far.

"Do you need numbers?" I said.

"Hmm?" He didn't look up, but I knew he was listening.

"For that part, there."

I pointed at a paragraph describing the link between hunger and poor school performance in America.

"You're making your point, but you don't have any details to drive it home."

"You think it's too vague?"

He looked at me now, his interest piqued.

"Well, your audience is mixed tomorrow, right? Between your regular voters and your big-spending potential donors?"

"Definitely."

"Well, if everyone's middle class to wealthy, the whole idea is probably just theoretical to them. They've heard about it, but they need to feel it in their gut to really get it. That's why you need details. Numbers. Something that they have to chew on."

Jackson stared ahead for a while, lost in thought.

"I think… I think I'd like your help, Rose," he said, running a hand over his chin. "Now you've got me wondering if I'm one of those people who doesn't feel it hard enough. And if I don't, how can I make them feel it?"

I chewed my lip. I always forgot that he was sheltered from the things the rest of us went through. He had such a good heart, it was easy to forget. But, he probably didn't even know the price of a gallon of milk. He didn't have to. He had people for that.

"Well, off the top of my head, I know that one out of every five kids is currently hungry in this country. So if your voters imagine their kids' soccer team, which usually has about ten players, two of those kids don't get enough to eat each week. They live in poverty that affects their daily lives and their health."

Jackson whistled low, typing notes at the bottom of his speech.

"I know that over nine million kids currently participate in a free lunch program because they can't afford a meal otherwise… and I also know that over ten million go without who need it, because the schools don't have the funding to feed them."

"Jesus."

"The kids who are getting those lunches, which are often all they'll eat that day, usually don't have a program to feed them over the weekend, and certainly not over summer vacation. That's when even the ones getting help slip through the cracks.

"A school in my neighborhood has a tradition called 'Pasta Monday' where they fill the kids up with huge portions each Monday because they know a lot of them haven't had a meal all weekend long."

Jackson was staring at me, his eyes pained, like he couldn't believe what I was saying.

"I… Christ. I mean, I knew the high level statistics, but I didn't know about Pasta Monday for God's sakes."

He pinched the bridge of his nose, then looked back up at me, shaking his head.

"You're right, these are the details I need. People know that hungry kids don't do as well in school, and that America needs better education if we're going to be a strong going forward, but... We don't see it, so we don't get emotional about it. We don't get passionate because it doesn't seem real."

"I know," I said. "It's hard to understand what you haven't lived through. Until it hits home, it's all just words. Especially here, you know? The disparity in this country feels invisible sometimes."

He typed, shaking his head, and I leaned on him, murmuring suggestions. As strange as it was, I was grateful that I did understand, so I could provide some perspective to a man like Jackson Pierce, someone who was in a place to affect change, but needed perspective. And as painful as it was, as hard and fucked up as parts of my life were, I knew good people like him needed me to guide them the rest of the way. To show them what was once invisible and bring it into the light.

The flight attendant refilled my wine glass, and I sipped it slowly, eventually falling asleep with my head on Jackson's shoulder, lulled by the sounds of him typing away, and the soft rumble of the engines.

"He's great up there, isn't he?"

Lucy whispered to me, leaning in as we watched Jackson's speech from beside the stage, looking out over the thousands who turned up in front of the courthouse to cheer him and show their support. People's faces were upturned, their eyes shining as they listened, clapping and whooping when he hit on his campaign promises, and now, rapt as he described the school my teens went to and the tradition of Pasta Monday.

"He really is," I said, smiling. "I just hope this speech doesn't backfire. We still don't have any info on the blackmailer, right?"

Lucy sighed, taking my arm, and shook her head, her red curls bobbing.

"Nothing. I mean, everyone in the campaign seems to think you two are really in love. My sister called, and Chase hasn't discovered anything, either. Whoever the person is, they are playing their cards mighty close to the vest. It sucks."

I nodded vigorously, and squinted at the people lining the stage behind Jackson, trying to read their faces. Lisa was talking amicably with a cameraman, gesturing toward Jackson as the crowd applauded, probably making sure he didn't miss the excitement of the rally goers reactions. Jackson's media guy and other key staff members stood, watching the crowd, watching him, and watching the members of the press, clamoring at the foot of the stage in turn. They seemed focused and professional, no one sneaking off to make a mysterious phone call or cutting-and-pasting letters out of a magazine into a threatening note.

I don't know what I expected.

The lawyer wasn't here, but why would he be? And if anyone from Ramsee's camp was there, they were definitely laying low. Besides, why would they show when they could just wait for the evening news to catch the highlight reel. Jackson's speech would tip whoever it was off that at least so far, he wasn't changing his platform.

The deadline listed in the threat was less than three weeks away, so I hoped we still had time before they did anything rash. But as I knew only too well, if they were desperate or greedy, you never knew what they would do. People like that were dangerous, especially if they knew you were trying to corner them.

Max and Lucy met Jackson and I for a meal in the park after his speech, all of us trying to stay far away from prying ears and eyes.

"I have to get back," Max said. "Father's going to have a stroke if I leave the company for more than a week."

"But I'll keep up the book club," Lucy said, grinning slyly. "If there's any gossip flying around, you know someone's going to let it slip after enough sangria."

"Thank you both," Jackson said. "I won't forget it."

"Isa said Chase is keeping in touch with his old friend, too. We'll call you if we unearth anything. Hang in there, Jacks."

Max patted his brother roughly on the back, and Jackson shook his hand. Lucy and I embraced.

"Call me if you ever need to talk," she said. "I mean it." She pointed a finger at me, smiling.

Despite my shyness, I grinned.

"Will do."

They walked away, hand in hand, and as I watched them, I wondered if what Jackson and I had was anything like what they did. If we ever could, after all of this was over.

"I need to get back to headquarters," Jackson said. "My driver will take you wherever you want to go."

He leaned down and kissed me, cupping my face in his hands.

"Let me know if you hear anything," I said. "Promise me, okay? I want to help if I can."

"I will, Rose. Now, keep an eye out for yourself. Be safe. I'll see you as soon as I can, but it will probably be late tonight."

He left with a reassuring smile, and I sighed, watching him walk down the path, back toward the stage and his milling staff. Despite the heat of the day, I shivered, a feeling of dread settling over me like a palpable chill.

It was the feeling of waiting for something to happen, but knowing that when it did, it would be like a bomb dropping, shattering everything in your life you cared about. If it wasn't Jackson's reputation and career, it would be the programs my kids relied on, and either one would hurt someone I loved. Hurt them so deeply they may never recover.

All because of one person, threatening him, threatening all of us, and for what? Some political gain? The whole thing filled me with anger, like a poison seeping into my bloodstream, each time I thought about it.

I walked toward the car, crossing my arms against the weight of my worry, trying to forget, for one moment, all that was at stake. Regina used to say that worries were like tits on a bull: udderly useless. But even now, that thought didn't cheer me like it used to.

When I sank back into the leather seat and the car pulled away from the curb, I realized my cheeks were wet. I swiped the tears away and looked out the window, praying that something would happen, and the hammer that hovered over all of us would never fall.

CHAPTER 26

I watched Rose cooking from the kitchen doorway, her back to me, and her arms covered in flour as she kneaded pizza dough. She chased my chef and staff away, insisting she enjoyed the hard work, and stood, moving her hips to a silent beat, headphone wires tucked expertly under the strap of her tank top and running down her back, out of the way.

I sighed, leaning against the doorframe.

Last night, work went late, all of us evaluating the media response to the rally, strategizing until the take out was cold, and the streets were quiet. I'd snuck into the master bedroom, and found Rose sleeping on one side of my bed, a nightlight glowing in the bathroom, guiding my way. A book was open on the bedspread beside her. I tucked it away and crawled beneath the covers, trying not to disturb her. The way her black hair fanned out like a messy halo on the pillowcase, the way her lips fell halfway open as she mumbled in her sleep, the way her dark lashes caressed her cheek, made me stay awake, watching her face and the rise and fall of her breasts beneath the sheet as she breathed.

I'd never watched a woman sleep before, had never even had one share this bed with me. The feeling of having her here, filling the empty space with her presence, made me ache in a way that wasn't altogether unpleasant. Was this what it was like? Was this what people talked about when they said they'd fallen in love?

When they couldn't imagine their life without the other person in it?

I had to leave again before the household awoke, and I kissed her parted lips softly. She sighed in a way that made my cock stir, but there was no time for that, as much as I wanted her. I tore myself away and dressed in my closet, before sneaking out the suite and shutting the door carefully behind me.

Now, I stole a moment, needing to see her, even if it was only for an hour before I had to get back to the office, to the campaign, to my life before any of this ever happened. Before she fixed herself in my mind as something necessary. Something required for me to feel normal. To feel at home in my own place.

I thought about the note I found this morning, in an envelope tucked beneath my keyboard.

```
The clock is ticking, Jackson,
and you're wasting time.

A friend caught your speech
and thought it could have used
some editing.

Two and a half weeks left
before it all comes crashing down.

Think about the cost—can you
do any good as a blacklisted disgrace?
Time to wake up, Jackson,
before the clock runs out
on your career.
```

What good could I do if I could never hold office? If no one would even listen to my politics? If everyone believed I was a pervert and a liar…

I didn't see anyone else standing up for education reform. I didn't see anyone else trying to raise funding for youth programs in this state, much less coming up with a way to pay for it that didn't involve burdening the middle class. Sure, my idea meant cutting wages for the top government officials, but did the Governor really need a special house, transportation, retirement funding, and six figures per year? Were the complimentary lunches and expense accounts really necessary to make things happen in those offices?

Somehow, I think the wealthy who could afford to run a campaign in the first place could do with fewer perks if it meant improving the community they represented. What was the point of governing if you took care of yourself over the needs of your people?

There had to be a way to make change happen from the inside, even if my hands were tied on certain issues. There had to be a way to influence people… to force things through even if I couldn't be as direct as I wanted to be.

I looked back at Rose, humming now as she dusted her wooden pizza peel with cornmeal, her hips still swaying to the beat.

The thing that haunted me, on top of everything else, was that if I was exposed, she would be, too. The kids that attended the wedding would know that she lied to them for money. That she sold herself to that Pierce guy, the guy who everyone knows is a deviant and a fraud. That's all they would hear, all they would think about, when the news came out.

She'd never get a chance to explain that it was all for them.

The thought of Rose losing the people she cared about the most because of my indiscretions was too much to bear. I'd stomached a lot in this business for the greater good, but the thought of Rose disgraced made my skin crawl. Was it even for the greater good, when we would both lose so much? Was sticking to my principles the higher road, or was I being a stubborn fool for not swallowing my pride and giving in to these demands?

Rose pressed out the dough, rolling it into wide circles, her arm muscles straining, her tank riding up, exposing a strip of lower back above her jeans.

All I knew was that this woman was someone I needed in my life. I'd do anything to protect her, to keep her with me, to show her I wanted to make her happy. The problem was, I didn't know what that was yet. I just didn't know.

I crossed the kitchen in a few long strides and scooped her up into my arms. She yelled in surprise, jerking the buds out of her ears and breathing hard. Her eyes widened as they met mine.

"Jackson?"

I took her mouth with mine, kissing her so hard it almost hurt, feeling her breath fill my mouth, capturing her tongue with my own. I needed her so badly, I couldn't even think. Needed to be with her, to feel her love, to know that we had this, here and now, and nothing could stop us.

I lowered her to the floor and knelt over her, peeling her tank top up over her head, and pushing her bra down under her breasts, displaying them on top of the lace, ready to be touched, sucked, worshipped.

She moaned against the cool tile as I lowered my mouth to her hot skin, my cock straining against my zipper so hard, I thought it might burst the seam.

When we finally came together, it was hard, frenzied. I couldn't control myself. Not now. She wrapped her silky thighs around me, squeezing me in a way that made my mind go black, the hot feel of her pussy wrapped around me, accepting me, tormenting me with its slick tightness, making me savage.

But even as she scratched my back, the bite of her nails making me pant, and even as I thrust into her, pinning her hips to the floor, our bodies slamming together with the force of our lovemaking, I felt her combine with me, her heart and mine beating as one, in the midst of a passion so intense it bordered on violence.

When I rolled over onto my back, she rode me like a fury, her hands holding my biceps in a vice grip as she bucked on top of me, her hair flying and those sweet breasts bouncing as she fucked me so hard she left bruises. When I thumbed her clit, I saw her bite her lip, her eyes brimming with tears as she fought against her own pleasure, waiting, waiting for me, for my command.

"Cum for me," I growled. "Now!"

The look of bliss in her eyes as she let go, arching her back and screaming as I pinched her in that hot little place, was something I'll never forget as long as I live.

"I love you," I said, barely audible beneath her wails of pleasure.

I gasped and shot my cum inside of her, holding her hips down to mine, grinding up into her as I filled her, feeling her squeeze me until I thought I might die there, wrapped in her gorgeous body, sucked dry until my heart couldn't take any more.

When I sat up and crushed her to me, feeling the flutter of her breathing against my neck, her hard nipples grazing my chest, I wondered if she'd heard me. If I'd meant her to hear me. What would happen if she did?

Neither one of us spoke as we sat together, joined on the kitchen floor, flour handprints covering our bodies, sweat clinging to our skin.

The timer buzzed above us, and we jumped together, then laughed. She climbed off me, leaving me feeling cold, my body still longing for her, wanting her again and again for as long as I lived.

I gathered my clothes and got ready to go back to work. There was a lot to be done, and no time to linger, as much as I wanted to.

The campaign was waiting, and the clock was running down.

CHAPTER 27

Jackson Pierce was keeping something from me.

In the days after we made love on the kitchen floor, I barely saw him. Things were picking up speed with the campaign, and when he wasn't at his headquarters, he was on one talk show or another, or giving a speech at a black tie dinner. I was by his side during events, trying my hardest to be a convincing wife, and even more, a friend, but it was hard.

He sent me gifts, left me little notes on the pillow, but it wasn't the same. I walked into the kitchen one morning, and froze when I saw the sky blue KitchenAid mixer, standing there with a bow on top and a crimson rose in a vase beside it.

How had he…?

And then I realized. That night at William Sonoma, so long ago now, he must have been watching me. He remembered me touching this mixer, and now it was here, an offering, with a note that just said "Thinking of you." It was wonderful, but at that moment, I'd rather have lunch with him then accept this beautiful gift. I felt ungrateful, guilt bubbling up inside of me as I ran my hands over it, thinking about that night and all that followed.

I missed him at night, falling asleep next to me the way he did in Jamaica, I missed having meals with him, laughing with him, sharing my days with him. But more than that, I felt him pulling away, and that, more than anything, frightened me.

Sometimes when we did find a moment together, there was an odd look in his eyes, like he was looking past me, thinking about something troubling him, and then he'd be back, his neutral mask sliding back into place, and I wouldn't know what to think.

At first I thought it was just the stress of trying to find information on the blackmailer, and coming up empty, or maybe the waiting, doing nothing, wondering if another note would appear or if he'd be exposed at any minute, since he hadn't rolled over yet and given into their demands.

Then, I found the second note.

I climbed out of bed to find him missing again, the sheets wrinkled beside me, the pillow still carrying the lingering scent of his cologne. I ran my hands over it, and sighed, then got up and pulled his dress shirt off the floor where he dropped it when he undressed in the dark. I wanted to feel close to him, to snuggle up inside something that smelled like him. As I buttoned it up, I noticed something peeking out of the shirt pocket. A card with typewritten lines—the same as the last threat.

Jackson hadn't said a word about it, though, not to me, at least, and as I read it, a pit formed in my stomach. Why wouldn't he tell me? I was in this as much as he was. Unless, he didn't want me to know.

I unbuttoned the shirt and tossed it back onto the floor, my eyes blurring with tears of frustration. Did he not trust me? Or was he just trying to protect me from the truth? Both thoughts upset me, both took me down the same shitty path. He didn't think of me as a partner, even though he knew his platform directly affected me. Affected the kids.

I know he had his brother to confide in, but his brother wasn't the one pretending to be his bride to make this all go away. His brother wasn't living in his home, waiting for the other shoe to drop, waiting for the thing he cared most about to be ripped away at any moment. Waiting to see the center shut down, and those kids going hungry again, wandering the streets after school, getting into trouble simply because they were fucking desperate.

I swore, and tucked the card back into the shirt pocket, then pressed palms over my eyes, trying to push back the tears. To comfort myself, even when there was no comfort to be found.

The tears became sobs, my body wracked as the stress worked its way into a cyclone inside of me, my worry breaking free, taking over, dropping me to my knees on the carpet. I wanted to tear up that expensive shirt of his, to rip the card, to make it all go away, but I sat, shuddering as I wept, wondering how on earth we'd ever get out of this goddamn mess.

A sob stuck in my throat, and my stomach turned over as I gasped for breath. I ran to the bathroom, and vomited, my sobs turning to coughs as my body expelled bile and water. When the heaving finally stopped, I sat on the edge of the tub, my head in my hands, my body shaking.

I had to get it together.

I needed to talk to Jackson about this. About everything. I needed to be in the loop on this, whether he wanted me there or not. Because even if he was trying to protect me from the truth, I needed to know what was happening to my neighborhood, my community, my kids. I needed to prepare myself for what I was going to tell them if everything we worked so hard for fell apart.

I got dressed in a hurry, my stomach still protesting, and drove my car into the city, heading for the campaign office. Hopefully he'd be there, and we could settle this matter before my imagination ran wild, and I assumed the worst about him.

Despite everything, I knew Jackson was a man who did the right thing, even if that thing was the hardest option of all.

I just hoped he wouldn't let me down.

CHAPTER 28

I sat in my office, the words of the last threat burning in my mind.

The rally, the deadline the blackmailer set forth, was in just two days, and I still had nothing to go on. Max and I talked briefly about going to the police, but that was just another way to make sure I was ruined when the media caught wind. Better to keep looking for clues, and at least be somewhat in charge of my own fate.

But whoever sent the threats remained aloof, not showing themselves aside from those ominous notes, left where too many people had access, but where they were sure to get straight into my hands. They knew exactly what they were doing.

I looked at the framed picture on my desk, the picture Lisa took at the wedding, of Rose laughing in my arms as we danced. God, she looked beautiful. Her smile, her soulful eyes, her hair swept back as she spun with me, looking at me like I was the only man in the world.

I picked it up for a moment, bringing her closer, studying her face as I went over what I planned to do.

It was all written out, but could I really give that speech? When I took the stage the day after tomorrow, could I really denounce my stance in a way that would satisfy the blackmailer, but still get me elected? It needed to be believable, but still likable if I was going to protect Rose. If I was going to be elected Governor and make amends in other ways.

It wasn't what I wanted, but I had to try, for her. I couldn't let her get dragged through the mud with me, no matter the cost. She worked too hard for too long. And maybe she could keep the center open with my private funding... Maybe, she would even forgive me.

Because I knew that even if I pulled this off, she might not want anything to do with me. Oh, she'd stay because of the contract, she wasn't someone who reneged on her obligations, but she might hate me because I broke my promises, to her and to my constituents.

But it was for the greater good. Her greater good. And right now, that would have to be enough.

I set down her picture and picked up the speech, skimming it for the fiftieth time.

I know I've spoken quite a bit about education reform and about creating a prosperous future workforce through community programs and funding for our schools. However, sometimes those of us with the best intentions can put the cart before the horse. In our rush to do what is right, we can get our priorities out of order, and that is just as irresponsible as doing nothing at all.

In that light, I'm no longer focusing on those policies, but instead am putting the full steam of my campaign toward the most important issues facing our community and our state: Tax reform and easing the burden on the middle class.

I grimaced, my stomach in knots reading over the words I'd written. It was nonsense, but sadly, I knew it would play well, and people would respond to the trigger words "tax" and "burden." People hated taxes, despite their necessity, and soon, with enough rhetoric, would forget their disappointment in me abandoning the other parts of my platform.

Who knows? Maybe they'd even like me better, now that I wasn't rattling so many cages.

I straightened the cards and put them in my jacket pocket, ready to rehearse them later, when the interns had gone home, and I had the office to myself. Until then, there was paperwork to do, and people to call.

A politician's work was never over.

Especially when all I wanted to do was go home and be with the woman I loved. Two more days, and it might all fall apart. I just hoped Rose would understand that I did it all for her.

CHAPTER 29

I parked outside the headquarters and sat in my car, watching staff and interns enter and exit, and cars rolling by; BMWs and Kia Rios, minivans and coupes. Shadows lengthened as I watched, waiting in my car, wondering what to say to the man I loved. The man who I worried didn't trust me.

Who didn't even know how I felt because I was too afraid to tell him.

And where did I stand in his eyes? Was I his lover? Or just a cover story? What was happening between us, really? Was I too caught up in the myth we'd created to see the truth? If so, I really was a stupid girl.

I drummed on the steering wheel, then flipped on the radio, twirling the knob past station after station, nothing feeling right, the music jarring to my ears. Finally, I got out of the car and walked to a small café across the street. I ate lunch and drank iced tea, my stomach still too angry for coffee. And I waited, my thoughts spinning, feeling more and more ridiculous for even driving here, for bothering Jackson when the deadline was so close and his workload was so heavy.

He must be under so much stress right now. I wondered how he'd deal with the controversy if nothing turned up in time. How he'd face the media. How he'd spin the fact that he lied about me to cover up his unsavory past. Would people understand? Would they forgive him? Or would they burn him at the stake?

I chewed my straw until the end was a twisted wreck of plastic, then got another and chewed it as well. I paid and walked around the block, going over what I wanted to say, and coming up with nothing again and again.

"Jackson, I know about the second card. Why didn't you tell me?"

"Jackson, what's the plan? What are you going to do when the blackmailer outs you?"

"Jackson... do you love me?"

What was there to say? It was all coming apart in two days, and when that happened, what would become of me? Of us? Would he honor the contract, so I could at least help the center, or would we both lose everything?

Was it selfish of me to think that? Am I a bad person for wondering about the money at a time like this?

Maybe.

The thought haunted me.

I just wanted to fall into Jackson's arms and tell him it would all be all right, even though I didn't know if I believed it. I just wanted to be with him during these next two days, by his side, both of us helping one another through the stress of waiting for the clock to chime midnight and the day of the rally to dawn.

When night fell, I finally summoned the courage to walk into the headquarters and confront him. Almost everyone was gone from front office, but Jackson's driver hadn't been called to pick him up, so he must still be working.

I made my way through the slap-dash cubicles of the phone bank, past the messy desks of his staff, toward the back office, and the light glowing through the blinds of Jackson's window.

"Goodnight, Mrs. Pierce."

I turned and waved at the last staff member walking out the door, a grad student whose name I couldn't remember, and sighed as the door closed behind him. Now was our chance to talk. I just hoped I'd say the right thing.

As I approached the door to the office, I heard the sound of Jackson's voice. He was talking to someone, or maybe on the phone, so I hung back, listening, waiting for a pause, so I wouldn't be intruding.

His voice rose, more powerful now, and in the smooth timbre he only used when he was speaking in front of an audience, one that practically dripped authority. And then it dawned on me. He was practicing his speech now that everyone had left. I smiled, shaking my head. It was funny to me that he'd be shy about such things, after so many weeks of events.

I took a deep breath, and raised my hand to knock.

"In that light, I'm no longer focusing on those policies…"

My hand froze, mid air, and I leaned in, frowning as I strained to listen.

"But instead am putting the full steam of my campaign toward the most important issues facing our community and our state: Tax reform and easing the burden on the middle class."

I recoiled, my hand falling to my side. This couldn't be right. This couldn't be the speech he was giving. This was all wrong… Totally and completely wrong. I should never have come here.

"Together, we can make a difference," he said. "On these issues we will take our stand for a stronger, more prosperous tomorrow for all Americans…"

A sob escaped my lips, half gasp, half cry of shock. This was really happening. Jackson was going to give in, give up his platform, everything that made him the man people believed in. Everything that made him the man I fell in love with.

His voice stopped, and I heard footsteps inside the office. The door pulled open, and then he was there, his eyes widening as he took in the look on my face.

"Rose? What are you doing here?"

I stared at him in disbelief, my lips curling into a snarl. Sadness twisted violently inside me into something that tasted a lot like rage. Rage that he would dare do this, that he would compromise himself like this, that he could make me love him and then slap me in the face. That he could be such a goddamn coward.

"How could you do this?"

My voice came out in a low hiss.

"Rose, you don't understand. I have to-"

"Have to? You have to? You don't have to anything you don't want to do!"

He reached for my arm, tried to pull me into his office, but I backed away.

"I don't have a choice."

"Because of your career, right?" I spat. "I understand, Jackson. I understand now. I see what kind of man you are. I see what I didn't want to see. God, I was so stupid."

It all came out in a rush, my words flowing like molten lava, burning him with each syllable.

"You know why I came here tonight? Huh?"

"Rose, listen."

"No! No more lying, Jackson! I trusted you. I came here tonight because I found the second threat, the note you hid from me, and now I know why. You never wanted to do the right thing. This whole time all you cared about was the goddamn power of your goddamn office. And you couldn't risk that, despite the fact that it meant giving up on all of your principles, of lying down and getting walked all over. You make me sick!"

His face fell, his eyes full of fire, too, but his expression reeking of shame. It made me want to hit him.

"I never lied to you."

"Really? Because you certainly kept this speech of yours a big fucking secret!"

He looked at the cards in his hand, then tucked them into his jacket.

"Don't you have anything to say?"

"You wouldn't hear me out even if I did," he said.

His eyes flicked up to mine, his mask back in place. He was closing down, shutting me out, keeping me at arm's length even now.

"Do you know why else I came here tonight, Jackson?"

I was breathing heavily, trying to control my anger.

"Why, Rose." His voice was flat, his hands limp at his sides.

"Because I knew I might lose you soon, and I didn't want things to change without letting you know... letting you know that I fell in love with you, Jackson."

His hands clenched, his eyes shining now, the veneer in place, but cracking.

"I loved you, Jackson," I said. "But now, I know what a fool I've been. How can I love a man I can't even respect?"

He looked like I'd dealt him a physical blow, his face crumpling. He opened his mouth to respond, maybe even to apologize, but I didn't want to hear it. If I let him talk now, he might suck me back in, and I was too angry, too hurt to let that happen.

I couldn't believe I'd let him trick me, let him lie to me and lure me, make me think I was special. He was just like everyone else in my life who'd let me down. He was just a snake in the grass, and if I brought him close, he'd only bite me again.

So I walked away, striding toward the door before he could respond, and slamming it closed behind me. I was too angry to cry, too sick with grief to yell. I slammed the key in my ignition and tore out of there, driving off into the night, not sure where I was going, except that it was far away from him.

My tires squealed as I hit the gas, driving away from Jackson Pierce as fast as the car would take me.

CHAPTER 30

"Where is she? Where's Rose?"

I burst into the foyer, almost sending Geoffrey flying as he reached for the door to let me in. He stared at me now, his glasses sliding down the bridge of his nose, looking at me as if I'd lost my mind.

"She left this morning to go see you, I believe," he said, straightening his jacket. "Is something amiss, Sir?"

"She... I..."

I stopped myself from shouting Yes, something's fucking amiss! and tried to think. I couldn't let on that everything was falling apart. Not in front of the staff. Not in front of anyone. For all I knew, Geoffrey was on the payroll of the blackmailer now. I couldn't let the cracks show. I still had 48 hours, and I needed every second.

"She left the office before me, and I just wanted to make sure she arrived back safely is all," I said, smiling in a way I hoped was disarming. "I guess I worry too much. She probably just stopped by a friend's before coming home."

"Of course, Sir," Geoffrey said.

He didn't raise an eyebrow. Maybe I was okay after all.

"I'll be in my study. Can you please make sure I'm not disturbed?"

Geoffrey bowed and headed off to the back staircase, I'm sure to alert the staff of my request. I climbed the main stairs two at a time, rushing to the privacy of my study and shutting the door tightly behind me.

I needed to talk to someone. Someone who understood the situation. I was about a second away from doing something stupid, and I needed a rational voice. My fist itched to break something, to punch through the drywall, to hurl an antique vase across the room. I balled it tight and went to the phone, dialing without thinking.

"Jackson?"

Max's voice filled my ear, and I took a deep breath before answering.

"Rose is gone. She's gone, Max, and I might have fucked things up so badly tonight that... that I...."

"What? Slow down, Jacks. Calm down. What happened?"

I went over to the decanter of whiskey and popped the stopper, then took a long draw, coughing as it went down wrong.

"I wrote a speech, a speech giving in, and she heard me, Max. She heard me, and I couldn't explain... I couldn't tell her it was to protect her..."

"Oh, shit."

"I know. I know! God, I'm such a fuck up. I can't believe I let it get this far. That I couldn't find this bastard and just fucking fix this."

"What are you talking about? Shut up for a second and listen, okay? None of us could fix this, Jacks. Between you, me, and all the power of Chase Enterprises, we couldn't find this guy. You are not alone here. This is not your fault."

"This is just like before. I need you to fucking fight my battles, and I still come out fucked..."

"Is this...? Is that what you're worried about? Your pride? Or is this about Rose?"

"Rose. Of course it's about Rose. Well... both, maybe. I just... How can she love a man she doesn't even respect, Max? I mean, Jesus..."

There was a silence on the other end of the line, and I took another swig of whiskey, the burning in my throat a soothing heat.

"So you love her."

I could hear the grin in his voice, and wiped a hand over my face.

"Yeah. I do. I do, and now I've lost her. But no matter what I did, she was going to be hurt. If our lie came to light, she might lose the kids. They're her whole world."

"But if you give in, you show her you don't care about your policies. Policies that would make a difference for those kids and thousands like them just in this city, much less the whole state. If they're her whole world, how is that protecting her?"

"I thought maybe… maybe I could do some good for them in another way. Once I got elected."

Max sighed, and I could practically see him rolling his eyes.

"Are you seriously that naïve? You really think the blackmailer would stop once you were in office? That they'd let you go back on your word without ruining you? You'd be their pet, and you know it."

I looked out the window, clutching the decanter like I was choking it, taking in my brother's words.

"I don't know, Max. No matter what I do, we're screwed."

"Okay, okay, stop the pity party," Max said. "Let me ask you a couple of questions, Jacks. You know that if you give in, you will be at the mercy of some scumbag who doesn't want reform, right? So, if you don't give in, what's the worst that happens?"

"If I go up there and give my stump speech for education, then the blackmailer makes good on their threats, the press finds out that I faked a marriage, and now they're printing stories about me being a lying pervert for the rest of eternity. I'm humiliated and all of my donors pull out, and my campaign is ruined. No one will back me, even as a lobbyist, and I'm blacklisted from politics for life. Rose is smeared in the media as some kind of fraudster, maybe even a sex worker by the meaner rags, and her kids lose all respect for her. She may even be banned from working at the youth center. Her life is screwed up forever, and it's all because of me."

Max sighed.

"Does she love you, Jackson? Does she feel the same way you do?"

I shook my head, looking out the window, my eyes filling with tears for the first time in years. I refuse to let them fall and took another swig.

"She said she did. Tonight. But not any more. Not now that I've shown my true colors."

"So, maybe you got that worst case scenario all wrong. Hear me out on this one."

"Okay?"

I frowned, wondering what he could possibly say to make this anything less than the catastrophe it was.

"Let's say you give the speech you want to give. The real speech, and you really stick it to the blackmailer, really nailing your previous points about poverty and education. Make it the best speech of your life. Then, when you're outed to the media, are tarred and feather, etc, you tell Rose you're sorry you couldn't do more for her, but that you're honoring the contract." He paused. "You are honoring it, right? I mean, you're still paying the poor woman?"

"Yes! What do you think I am, some kind of-"

"Okay, just checking. So, you pay her, and you let her know that despite this whole circus, you love her, you always loved her, and if she'll have you, you'll spend the rest of your life making it up to her."

I don't know if it was the liquor, or Max's words, but some of the weight on my shoulders lifted, and I breathed out slowly. An idea formed, an idea that held with it a grain of hope.

"I could set up a foundation," I said. "I could set up a foundation in her name on top of the five million so that youth center would always have funding. We could provide food, mentor programs... scholarships..."

"Well, I just meant you shouldn't always look for the doom and gloom. I mean-"

"The Rose Turner Foundation. Then, even if she will never forgive me, at least I know she can still do what she loves. That she'll be all right. That the kids will be taken care of, even if I can't make a difference through politics. I could help run it, if she'd let me."

"Slow down, Jacks. I just meant-"

"Thank you, Max," I said, energy surging through me. "Thank you so much, I mean it. You and Lucy. You ought to marry that girl, you know? Okay, great talking to you."

I slammed the phone down, and dropped the decanter. I headed for my laptop and slapped my palms together. There was no more time to feel sorry for myself, or to worry about bruised pride.

I had a speech to write.

I called downstairs and asked the kitchen staff to bring me coffee so strong the spoon stood up on its own. It was going to be a long night.

I smiled, typing furiously, thinking of her. Thinking of my beautiful Rose.

CHAPTER 31

I stood in line at the pharmacy, my stomach in knots, thinking about the fight I had with Jackson. How could I not have seen this earlier? I'd promised myself and Regina I'd be careful, that I would guard my heart, but here I was, my eyes red and itchy from crying all night in my foster mom's apartment, my face buried in the crochet throw on her fold-out couch.

This morning, she offered to tear his arms off for me, but I just shook my head, my nose running like a faucet, and apologized until she told me to hush up and eat my hash browns. I barely had a forkful before I couldn't stand the smell and had to leave the table.

No one should be under this much stress. I just hoped above anything else that I was wrong right now. That this all would pass, and I wouldn't have to make the hard decisions. I just wanted this all to be over, so I could go on and live my life, free from the likes of Jackson Pierce.

I heard Regina's voice as she told me it would all work out, running her fingers through my hair the way I'd loved as a teenager, unable to sleep, afraid of the nightmares that would come.

At least there was one person I could trust in my life, besides myself. No matter what, I wasn't alone, and that was something.

I'd be okay, even if right now, it felt like I'd never feel normal again without him by my side. I hated him and I loved him, the emotions clashing and blending, melting together until I couldn't tell what I felt, only that I was hollow inside, scooped out, and I needed to be whole again.

I knew I would be. But it would be a long, long time.

Jackson Pierce had done a number on me when he broke my trust. I would never forget, and I would never make the same mistake again. There were some things I just couldn't forgive.

CHAPTER 32

Rose didn't come home last night or the night before, but I wasn't worried. I knew her mother lived in the city, and that she had friends from the center. She would be safe, and right now, that was all that mattered.

But as I went over the cards in my hand, mouthing the words of my new speech, I wished I knew where she was. That despite our falling out, she'd show up, that she'd be in the crowd, against all odds, all common sense. That she could see this live, instead of later, televised, spliced up against the news of the breaking scandal sure to follow.

"Two minutes, Jacks," Lisa said, peeking into my canvas tent behind the stage. "You're going to do great out there. Got your speech?"

"Sure," I said.

She helped proof the previous one, but not this one, written in a fevered state the night I called Max, and perfected the next day as I poured over the words, scratching out whole sentences and adding new ideas, words I remembered Rose saying as we flew back from our honeymoon, words I heard at the center, words of my own, conveying how deeply seeing the poverty up close with her changed me. How it opened my eyes, and now I needed the voters to stand with me, to make a better world through hard work and awareness of the community's needs, needs that were all but invisible until you knew where to look.

Now, I tucked the cards into my jacket pocket, and showed Lisa my most winning smile. She gave me the thumbs up and left, yelling at the lighting people to make sure the spotlight didn't have cool tones, as those clashed with my makeup.

I breathed deeply, waiting for my cue, for the moment that would define the rest of my life. Was I ready for what came next? For the humiliation? The accusations? My sex life splattered all over the news again for all to see and judge?

I imagined Rose, the look on her face when I told her about creating a foundation in her name... when I asked her to accept the position of CEO there, to make sure it was kept honest and efficient throughout the years. To help me build something that would do real, lasting good.

The thought steadied me. Centered me.

"This is for you," I said.

I brushed off my suit and took a deep breath. It was now or never.

I walked out of the tent, ready to give the speech of my life, and face the consequences with my head held high.

CHAPTER 33

I walked along the boulevard, past boutiques and cafes, my thoughts a jumbled mess. I'd avoided Jackson for two days, but today was the day of his speech. The day I didn't want to think about, but I couldn't banish from my mind.

I felt like a zombie, walking aimlessly, needing to get away from the apartment, but not knowing where to go, restless and alone. Should I confront Jackson again? Try to stop him? But if I did, what more was there to say? He was giving in to the blackmailer to save his own skin. It was clear what kind of man he was, and I wanted no part in his twisted games.

A couple of people stood in front of a store window, watching the flat screens displayed there, some showing the newest action movie to hit BluRay, but one tuned in to the rally happening in the park, just a few blocks from where I stood. I slowed down and stopped at the sound of Jackson's voice.

Keep walking, Rose. You know what he's going to say.

But my stubborn feet stayed planted. Maybe I just needed to hear it myself, to watch him betray his principles in front of the crowd, to watch as he threw away the things we both held dear as if they were nothing.

He was mid-sentence when I stopped, saying something about a budget. I watched him take a sip of water and continue.

"That's why if you allow me the privilege of being your Governor, I will forgo my salary, forgo the house and transportation, which are usually perks of the job, and make cuts to the spending the top state officials use on office luxuries. They are unnecessary, and unconscionable when there are children still going to bed hungry in this very city, and in cities like this all over the country."

I gasped and moved closer to the screen. The people beside me stared, then moved away, whispering, but I barely noticed.

"Many have called my plan for education reform too aggressive. Many, like my opponent, have said it's too little, too late. But I say if these programs help even one percent of the children in this community that don't have enough to eat, that go to class hungry and unprepared, that start at a disadvantage because of their social class, and not because of their intelligence or the effort they put forth... if these programs help even a handful of those children receive the basic provisions they need to be successful, then it is worth it. It is worth it because those kids are our future—the scientists of tomorrow we need to push progress forward, the doctors and entrepreneurs, the economists, the teachers that shape the generation after that.

"If we don't invest in our children now, if we can't even level the playing field by making sure they start their school day free of fear, instead of hungry and distracted and beaten down by circumstances they can't control, then we're not the people I thought we were.

"We can do this if lawmakers are ready to make the right decisions, if the people you elect to represent you are willing to give up some perks in order to fund these programs for the disadvantaged, if we pull together to create a state that lights the way for change across this great nation. We can do this. Together. We can do the right thing to make sure the next generation flourishes... and ensure our future is a bright one."

I shook my head, tears rolling down my cheeks. I couldn't believe this. He had the speech written before, and now... Now, everything was different. He was giving everything up, everything he'd worked so hard for—his career, his ambitions, his dreams—and I knew, in that moment, that he was giving it all up for me.

I understood his heart then as well as I understood my own. Jackson was making this sacrifice to prove to me he was the man I thought he was all along. The speech was a love letter, a declaration to me that he didn't care what happened, as long as I knew he was a man of principle. A man who took a stand for what was right, no matter the cost to himself. The kind of man I could spend the rest of my life with.

Suddenly, everything was clear, like a light shining down on me, sunlight burning away all the clouds of doubt and grief that shadowed me for days. I needed to get down there, needed to be with him when the inevitable happened, and the blackmailer brought everything tumbling down.

He needed me, and I needed him. It was as simple as that. Nothing had ever been simpler in my life.

I ran to the curb and yelled, waving for a cab. I just prayed I could get there before all hell broke loose.

The crowd was applauding when I approached, Jackson waving and smiling onstage. It was over, but was I too late?

I pushed my way through the throng, jostled by people cheering and whistling. I heard a couple of people booing, and the hair on the back of my neck stood on end. I knew there were always people who came to rallies to heckle, but today, I was on high alert.

I was almost to the stage when I heard Jackson announce he had time for a brief Q&A. The press moved forward, pushing me back, cameras flashing and hands waving, each of them clamoring to be the first.

Jackson answered one woman's question about his stance on the construction of a new bridge while I struggled toward the side of the crowd, trying to make my way to the staff area where I could find him afterwards. A male reporter began his question, and I froze in my tracks. From his tone, I knew—it was starting. I pushed harder, fighting to get closer.

"My office received a tip that your marriage to Ms. Turner is in fact a fraud—a business arrangement designed to distract from the unsavory rumors circulating in the press a few weeks ago. How do you respond to these very serious allegations?"

People in the crowd gasped, and the sound of people whispering to one another swelled like a wave. Cameras flashed again and again as Jackson cleared his throat. I pressed forward, but tripped as a reporter shuffled past me, hitting my knee hard on the ground. I swore and struggled to my feet.

"I would respond that those allegations have no grounding whatsoever, and that whoever started that rumor must have an ulterior motive. The notion that my marriage to Rose Turner is anything but genuine is extremely offensive."

Reporters' voices rose, each yelling for attention, but the accuser's voice soared above them, cutting them off.

"Isn't it a little too convenient that just as you're implicated in a sex scandal, you marry some girl no one's ever heard of? Someone who just happens to be a pillar in the community? It's being said you paid Ms. Turner to lie for you, and that you're not even romantically involved with the woman!"

I reached the edge of the stage just as Jackson responded. I waved, frantically trying to get his attention.

"You can't help when you fall in love," he said.

"What proof do you have that you're even sharing a bed, Mr. Pierce? If this is just some business arrangement to pad your image, the public has a right to know!"

I made a noise of disgust at that, but Jackson, miraculously, kept his cool.

"As for proof of our sexual involvement, what goes on in my bedroom is strictly between me and my wife. You can't possibly-"

"I think what happens in your bedroom is exactly what got you into this mess in the first place," the reporter quipped, interrupting. "And now you're lying to voters to cover up your sick little scandal. You have a responsibility to air the truth, Mr. Pierce! Voters have a right to know who they're electing!"

The crowd grew louder, people shouting at the stage. The reporters pressed closer, cameras rolling. Jackson tried to quiet the crowd, but other members of the press were demanding he answer the questions.

"Enough!" I shouted. "I'm his wife!"

People's shouts died down as I yelled into the portable mic I snatched from the side of the stage. Murmurs rose and fell as everyone in the crowd vied for a better look as I climbed the steps to the stage, Jackson's staff members waving security away from blocking my path.

"I'm his wife," I said, holding a stitch in my side as I walked to his side.

A squeal of feedback sounded, and I snapped the mic off now I was next to his podium, his microphone.

Jackson shook his head at me, his eyes pleading with me.

"Rose…"

I pointed at the reporter who first accused Jackson, my eyes narrowing.

"Since you insist on intruding into our very private, personal lives, let me put your mind at ease. Jackson and I are very much in love, and have been since the moment we met at the youth center where we both volunteer. From the moment I saw him, I knew. He was the one I'd been waiting for all my life."

I took his hand in mine, and Jackson looked at me, his eyes still full of worry.

"Why should we believe you? You've been paid off to lie for him! It's all one big spin to keep us from the truth. Sources say you haven't even consummated this bogus marriage, which means it's not even legal!"

Gasps and shouts came from the crowd now. Someone threw a bottle, and it exploded as it hit the edge of the stage with a crash, showering the ground with glass. Things were getting out of control.

Enough was enough. I dug into my purse. This had gone too fucking far, and I wasn't going to take it any more.

"I'm sorry I have to do this here instead of in private like I'd planned, but you've given me no choice. I DO have proof that the marriage is real, and that in your own, cheap words, we've consummated it. It's as legal as it gets, and how dare you suggest otherwise."

I glared at the reporter in a way that would blister paint, and raised my arm high above the crowd. Sunlight glinting off the pink, plastic stick in my hand.

"I'm two weeks pregnant! Jackson and I are expecting a baby."

A moment of silence fell, and then the crowd burst into an uproar, the reporter's protests drowned out by cheers and whoops of joy, along with so much yelling from the press, it was almost deafening. Everywhere I looked, camera flashes burst, and rally goers texted furiously on their phones.

The cat was officially out of the bag.

Jackson tugged on my hand, and I looked up into his eyes, now brimming with tears, the expression on his face one of awe and joy and disbelief, all rolled into one.

"Are you… are we…?"

I nodded and showed him the plus sign on the pregnancy test.

"During the honeymoon. I was late afterwards, but I didn't know for sure until today."

He pulled me close as reporters clamored beneath the stage and security tightened up, hemming us in.

"We're going to have a baby, Jackson."

He knelt then, and pressed a kiss to my stomach, looking up at me in a way that made all the pain of the last few days melt away.

"I love you, Rose," he said. "I've never loved anyone so much."

He rose to his feet and kissed me, gathering me up in his arms. The crowd went wild, whooping and cheering below us, and I realized his mic was still picking everything up. I laughed, suddenly giddy, not caring who heard, because Jackson Pierce loved me, and his baby was growing inside of me.

"I love you, too, Jackson."

I kissed him again, tears streaming down my cheeks, almost unable to believe that one person could be this relieved, this happy, without bursting at the seams.

"No more questions for today," Jackson shouted to the crowd, grinning in a way I'd never seen before.

Reporters protested, and the rally goers whooped, giving him the thumbs up.

The mask was gone, and the real Jackson here, his joy apparent for anyone who had eyes to see. Without another word, he scooped me off my feet and into his arms. I squealed and held on, letting him carry me off the stage as camera flashes followed us, along with the noise of celebration from the crowd behind.

Music swelled as he carried me down the stairs, Jackson's upbeat exit track surrounding us, drowning out everything but the feel of his arms around me, holding me close, carrying me and our child away from prying eyes, and into the waiting car.

When we were alone, he kissed me again and again, first my lips, then my cheeks, my neck, my breasts. He was breathless, his eyes shining fiercely.

"It's true?" He asked, looking up at me in a way that made my heart ache in my chest. "Please tell me that wasn't just a stunt?"

"It's true," I said, smiling as I ran my hands through his hair.

His face lit up, and he pulled me onto his lap, cradling me in his arms, stroking my back like he couldn't get enough of me.

"Was… Was what you said true, too?" I said.

He bit my lip, and I laughed.

"Which part? The part where I stopped being an idiot and told you how I've felt about you for weeks now?"

"Mmm," I agreed. "That part."

He ran his tongue over my bottom lip in a way that made me moan, teasing me, before capturing me in another long, sensual kiss. I felt him swelling against me, his hardness rubbing my ass through his pants.

"I love you, Rose. I'm so sorry I didn't tell you before. I'm sorry about everything."

I stopped his lips, tasting him right back. His cock twitched beneath me.

"Shhh. You were trying to do the right thing. You always do. I should have trusted you."

"It was you. I couldn't stand to see you ruined, and for a while, I thought that meant giving in to save your reputation. You made me realize what a fool I'd been..."

"You made me so proud today, Jackson. I knew that was for me up there. That you were ready to give it all up because you wanted to show me who you really are. What kind of man you've always been."

He brushed my hair back, staring deep into my eyes.

"I mean it, Rose. I've never loved anyone the way I love you. You make me proud every day, make me want to be better just by watching you. The way I feel when I'm with you is indescribable. It's so right... I need you in my life. I want you with me, always."

He nibbled my neck, and I shivered in his arms.

"Rose?"

"Yes," I breathed, planting a soft kiss on the corner of his mouth.

"Will you marry me? I mean, stay married to me? Will you please, really, be my wife?"

I touched his cheek, looking into his eyes, shock turning into joy as I soaked up the look there telling me everything I needed to know. Jackson Pierce loved me with all his heart, and I realized, I couldn't live without him, either. Not for one more minute. Not when I could be with him forever, by his side, his wife and love, the real Mrs. Pierce.

"Yes, Jackson. God, yes."

"Oh, Rose..."

We came together, me straddling him, him holding my hair, kissing me so hard I tingled from my head to my toes, my body responding to him like never before.

We never did make it back to the rally, but I'm his campaign staff understood. After all, us newlyweds valued our private time.

And if the driver heard anything on the ride back, he was nothing but professional when we finally arrived back at Jackson's home.

My home now, too. I supposed I had to get used to that. I was going to marry the love of my life. We were going to be a family, the family I always wanted, but never thought I'd have. I didn't think the day couldn't get any better, but as Jackson carried me over the threshold, much to the butler's confusion, I remembered one thing that might just put it over the top.

I absolutely couldn't wait to see the news tonight and watch the reports roll in on Jackson Pierce's eventful rally. It was going to be sensational.

CHAPTER 34

"Why'd you do it, Lisa?"

I sat across from her in my office, blinds drawn, the bustle of the office muffled behind the closed door.

"What on earth are you talking about?" She pushed her glasses up and smirked. "Despite your best efforts to screw it up, we came out okay yesterday. It's all over the news blogs. Everyone's talking about your wife's big announcement."

I stared at her, letting the silence stretch. I leaned back in my chair, watching her. She fiddled with the bottom hem of her blazer, her eyes flicking up to mine, then down again.

"I'm not sure what you're getting at here, Jacks. You know I'm on your side. I made you what you are, here. You should be thanking me."

Now she stared at me, hardly blinking, her eyes cold, even while she smiled, trying to throw me off.

"All I know is when we tracked down that reporter--you know, the one who accused me at the rally?--he had no problem spilling the beans about who paid him to call me out in front of the crowd."

"Oh?"

Her eyes darted toward the door.

"Yes, indeed. And you know what he said, Lisa?"

"No, Jacks. Lay it on me."

She folded her arms, her foot tapping as she met my gaze.

"He said it was you."

Her face fell, her expression flashing into a sneer, then back again, and she fought to remain composed.

Gotcha, Lisa.

"Maybe he's a liar."

"Maybe we both know it will go easier for you if you cut the bullshit, Lisa."

Her mouth snapped shut, and she shook her head, her eyes glinting like a cornered rat.

"But why did you do it? Why would my own campaign manager want to ruin me?"

She leaned forward, her eyes burning into mine.

"You really want to know, Jackson? Huh? You really want to know why the fuck I would do something like that?"

"I do. I trusted you."

"Maybe it's because I knew I was going fucking nowhere tagging along you're your sorry ass. If you're elected Governor, then what? You'd never move up, never go to Congress, never, God forbid, have enough balls to run for President. It's a one way fucking ticket to Losertown with you and your bleeding-heart causes."

"Why'd you come on board in the first place, if I'm such a dead end, Lisa?"

"You're young, you're handsome. Most like you are easily swayed. Easy to control. They do what they're fucking told so they can get ahead. But not you, not fucking Golden Boy Jacks Pierce. You just had to have a conscience, and you know what that makes you, buddy boy? Goddamn weak. You don't have the balls to do what needs to be done. I didn't build my reputation playing it safe in the kiddy pool with chicken shits like you."

I sighed, and stared at her, the woman I trusted with my career for so long.

"So if I'm weak, who's strong, Lisa? Tell me that much."

"Ramsee," she said, her voice low and deadly. "I knew if I talked you into this marriage schtick you'd either fall in love with the girl or get cold feet. Either way, I could say I did everything in my power to help, while watching you sink like a fucking rock."

"You'd come out looking clean."

"Exactly. Then, when you screwed it up and lost, I'd be free to go work for some new talent. Talent who would know I was the only one that gave you a half a chance in the first place. That it was me who gave Ramsee's campaign a run for his money. Until naïve little Jacks decided to fuck over his life for a piece of doe-eyed, hippy-ass pussy."

I grinned, running my hand over my chin.

"Well, Lisa. I hope you realize you're fired."

She scoffed, her eyes narrowing.

"Fuck you, Jackson. I'll be back at work in week, tops. Guarantee it. I don't need your stamp of fucking approval to get a job in this town."

"Language, Lisa. Your mouth has already gotten you into enough trouble for one day, don't you think?"

"What do you-"

The door burst open, and two police officers entered the room, both of them flanking Lisa. She yelled, trying to get out of the chair, but one of them was already cuffing her, wrenching her arms behind her back.

"Lisa Stoneworth, you're under arrest for blackmail, slander and corporate espionage. You have the right to remain silent…"

She shouted over them, threatening me, asserting that the charges would never stick, but fell silent as I raised up my shirt, showing her the wire strapped to my chest.

"Goodbye, Lisa. Good luck finding work when news of your arrest hits the news sites."

It turned out that even though Chase Drake couldn't find the blackmailer, he did have friends in high places. Friends who were more than happy to set up a sting operation using local law enforcement.

I saluted as the cops dragged her out of the office, her lips pulled back in a snarl. I followed them out, and smiled at Rose, leaning against the water cooler, watching the door with a smile.

"Got it all?"

"Oh, yeah," I said. "We got it. I hope Lisa likes orange, because she's going to be wearing a jumpsuit for a long, long time."

I put my palm on her stomach and looked into her eyes, the knowledge that she not only wanted to be with me, but that soon, we'd be raising a baby of our own, still enough to take my breath away.

"And more importantly, she won't meddle in our lives ever again. It's over."

She put her hand over mine, her warmth filling me with a love so intense, I didn't know if one man could hold it all.

"Then, what do you say to taking the day off, Mr. Pierce?"

She grinned up at me, her eyes full of mischief.

"Why, Mrs. Pierce... are you trying to seduce me?

"Do I need to try?"

She ran her fingers over mine, her touch doing more than enough to make up my mind.

"I'll be back tomorrow," I shouted to the room at large.

An intern rolled his eyes, and my media guy laughed, shaking his head.

"You've earned it," he said. "We can hold down the fort for one day, Jackson."

I bent down and threw Rose over my shoulder, smiling as she yelled and kicked, and carried her out of the office, the whistles of my staff following us out into the street.

CHAPTER 35

"You may now kiss the bride."

Jackson's lips met mine, and the wind picked up, blowing my veil around us as I sighed into him, enjoying this moment, the kiss that would change my life forever.

When we broke apart, the two construction workers we'd asked to witness clapped and cheered, tossing birdseed at us as the pastor announced us man and wife. This ceremony was private, just for the two of us, in a place that we both decided was the perfect place to begin our lives together.

My husband brushed my veil back, and smiled, tears shimmering in those dark eyes of his. He ran a hand over my stomach, rounding now as I neared the end of my second trimester.

"How do you like your wedding gift?"

He held me close at his side, and I took in the site of the building project, now just beams and concrete, that would soon become the Rose Pierce Foundation. When Jackson told me his plans, I didn't believe him at first, didn't believe that all of my dreams could come true without me paying some kind of terrible price. But then I thought about all we'd been through, all I'd been through, and a peace I'd never known settled over me.

Just as terrible things happened in this world, good things also happened. Everything happened under the sun, and just as there was darkness, there was always light as well. I'd just been in the darkness so long, I didn't know what to do when the sun shone down on me.

"It's perfect," I said. "Better than I ever imagined."

We stood under a scaffolding, using it as a make-shift arch, decorated with vines and candles, the unfinished room more beautiful than any chapel I'd ever stood in. I'm glad I never imagined my wedding as a child, because it never could have lived up to this. Just Jackson and I, in the place where our future would blossom and flourish, seeing our dreams built around us, even as we joined our hearts together.

When the license was signed, a new one with new names, since Jackson insisted on replacing the one already filed, the pastor and workers left us to ourselves, but not before turning on the sound system as they filed out.

Jackson and I toasted, him watching me carefully as I tried my first glass of Dom Perignon, his face lighting up as I savored it, rolling over my tongue. When the first notes of Kiss from a Rose began playing, I laughed, taking the hand he extended and letting him draw me close.

We danced in the flickering candle light, and I imagined the feet that would walk across this same floor in years to come, the joys that would be experienced here, the people who's lives would be transformed along with our own.

I held Jackson close, and let my tears fall, knowing that this was just the beginning, that there was so much for us to experience together, so much change still to come, so many firsts and so many struggles, but above all, so much love to give. To share with one another as husband and wife.

Our lips met, and soon, our kisses became urgent, our hands wandering over one another's bodies. Jackson, led me into the other room, and I laughed as I took in the elaborate display of tea lights, covering every surface, every saw horse and block of unfinished wood, and the wrought-iron bed set in the middle of it all, white canopy billowing in the breeze coming in from the open roof.

He really did think of everything, didn't he?

As our bodies entwined in this place where our pasts became our future, I cried out, my happiness spilling over into ecstasy as he made me his own. And this time, when we fell asleep together, I knew. I'd never be alone again.

I was loved, and I would love in return with all my soul, and no one could ever take that away from me.

I finally found a home, in Jackson Pierce's arms.

The End

ABOUT THE AUTHOR

Delilah Fawkes is the best-selling erotic romance author of "The Billionaire's Beck and Call" series, selling more than 150,000 e-books in 2012.

She's known for sizzling romances with red hot alpha males you'll fall in love with and strong women who capture their hearts. If you like your romance gripping, fast-paced, and dripping with sinful love scenes, you've got to check out what Delilah has to offer.

Delilah Fawkes always delights in bringing you the very best in erotic and contemporary romance!

For more Delilah Fawkes stories, visit her blog or check out her author page.

BONUS MATERIAL

*Love billionaire alpha males? Check out this sneak peak of LUSH
CURVES, a sensual, exotic romance from Delilah Fawkes:*

The moment I saw her, I knew she was something special.

I wanted to laugh when I saw her bending over that coffee spill,
looking back at me in such a vulnerable position, but something in
those deep, black eyes and, let's face it, the arresting sight of her
bum pointing straight at me, made me clear my throat and look
away before she got the wrong idea. I wanted her, my body reacting
to hers, but I had business to attend to. And I certainly didn't need
to be leering at any employees.

But when Martin introduced us, and I felt her small hand in
mine, I couldn't help but feel the connection, couldn't deny the
chemistry between us. With her flowing, black hair and gorgeous
skin, she was one of the most beautiful women I'd ever seen, and
my thoughts wandered to the strictly unprofessional.

What would her body look like set free from her business attire?
What would those gorgeous curves of hers look like clad only in a
teeny, tiny Bond Girl bikini?

Now, standing on the deck of my yacht, I marveled at her
bravery. That a person with no experience modeling would have the
confidence to get up there and give it a go was impressive, to say
the least. I asked her to do it--Hell, I nearly begged her--but I don't
know if I could have done the same, if she's asked me to don a
Speed-o in front of a wanker like Martin, not to mention the rest of
the crew.

Aolani was something else. Something remarkable. And even
though I knew I shouldn't get involved, I wanted to know more
about her.

"Um... Where should I stand?"

Aolani's voice cut through my thoughts. She stood near the
cabin, the anxiety in her eyes as clear as day, twisting her hands

together in front of her body. That beautiful body that should never be covered up.

Martin opened his mouth to answer, probably to tell her to quit fidgeting, but I spoke first.

"Would you please join me by the railing?"

She glanced at Martin's frown, then nodded to me, obviously relieved I'd be giving the instructions. Martin fumed next to me, but I'd deal with him later. It was too important that she remain calm and comfortable in order to get the shot right.

She wasn't one of his models, who cut their teeth on the abuse of bastards like him snapping away. It was painfully obvious she didn't know how beautiful she was, or what she was capable of. She didn't know what I saw when I looked at her.

She was next to me now, looking up at me with those almond eyes, drawing me to her with that inexplicable tug I felt whenever she was near. I could smell the scent of coconut in her hair, and I couldn't stop my eyes from traveling downward, over her ample cleavage held perfectly by the cups of her white bikini. My eyes traveled back up to hers, and I cleared my throat.

I had to remain professional.

"I'm picturing you leaning over the railing, Aolani, your elbows resting gently on the wood as you look out to sea. Can you try that for me now?"

She nodded and leaned over, clasping her hands together as she gazed out. I assessed her posture, trying to keep my breathing steady as my gaze slid over her tiny waist and flat belly to the rounded swell of her full hips... and that arse that made my cock stir in my trousers every time I saw it...

"Roll your hips back a little and arch your back, lass," I said. "It will show you off more."

She looked at me, her brow furrowing. "Are you sure you want that?"

She looked down, and I could see her cheeks coloring. I wanted to reach out and stroke her cheek, to tell her she had nothing to be afraid of, but I didn't know how she'd react. I settled for brushing her hair off her shoulder, and noticed her sharp intake of breath when my fingers grazed her skin.

"Absolutely," I said. "I want to capture those beautiful curves of yours. Soften your gaze as you look out, like you're seeing everything that you dream of, just over the horizon... Do you know how I mean?"

She chewed her lip and glanced down at my hand, still resting on her shoulder, but didn't pull back.

"I think so," she said. "I'll give it a try."

She pushed her hips back ever-so-slightly and opened her shoulders, arching her back. I sucked in a breath, and motioned for Martin to come over quickly. The lighting crew followed, hastily setting up their gear.

"Now, Aolani," I said. "Gaze toward the horizon."

The wind kicked up, whipping her hair back behind her. Her expression took on the quality of a dreamer, her face relaxed and serene as she looked out over the harbor waves. In that moment, I would have given anything to know what she dreamed about--what kind of vision for her future made her look so peaceful, so hopeful... and so utterly beautiful.

Martin's camera snapped away, and he started his spiel, telling her to adjust slightly this way and that until he had every angle he wanted captured. But I knew we'd gotten what we needed with that first shot.

Aolani Kahale was a natural.

7814627R00116

Made in the USA
San Bernardino, CA
17 January 2014